# A warning to the curious
## And other ghost stories

**M. R. James**

**A warning to the curious and other ghost stories**

The present edition is a reproduction of previous publication of this classic work. Minor typographical errors may have been corrected without note; however, for an authentic reading experience the spelling, punctuation, and capitalization have been retained from the original text.

ISBN: 978-1-64439-900-2

# CONTENTS

# A WARNING TO THE CURIOUS

The place on the east coast which the reader is asked to consider is Seaburgh. It is not very different now from what I remember it to have been when I was a child. Marshes intersected by dykes to the south, recalling the early chapters of Great Expectations; flat fields to the north, merging into heath; heath, fir woods, and, above all, gorse, inland. A long sea-front and a street: behind that a spacious church of flint, with a broad, solid western tower and a peal of six bells. How well I remember their sound on a hot Sunday in August, as our party went slowly up the white, dusty slope of road towards them, for the church stands at the top of a short, steep incline. They rang with a flat clacking sort of sound on those hot days, but when the air was softer they were mellower too. The railway ran down to its little terminus farther along the same road. There was a gay white windmill just before you came to the station, and another down near the shingle at the south end the town, and yet others on higher ground to the north. There were cottages of bright red brick with slate roofs... but why do I encumber you with these commonplace details? The fact is that they come crowding to the point of the pencil when it begins to write of Seaburgh. I should like to be sure that I had allowed the right ones to get on to the paper. But I forgot. I have not quite done with the word-painting business yet.

Walk away from the sea and the town, pass the station, and turn up the road on the right. It is a sandy road, parallel with the railway, and if you follow it, it climbs to somewhat higher ground. On your left (you are now going northward) is heath, on your right (the side towards the sea) is a belt of old firs, wind-beaten, thick at the top, with the slope that old seaside trees have; seen on the skyline from the train they would tell you in an instant, if you did not know it, that you were approaching a windy coast. Well, at the top of my little hill, a line of these firs strikes out and runs towards the sea, for there is a ridge that goes that way; and the ridge ends in a rather well-defined mound commanding the level fields of rough grass, and a little knot of fir trees crowns it. And here you may sit on a hot spring day, very well content to look at blue sea, white windmills, red cottages, bright green grass, church tower, and distant martello tower on the south.

As I have said, I began to know Seaburgh as a child; but a gap of a good many years separates my early knowledge from that which is more recent. Still it keeps its place in my affections, and any tales of it that I pick up have an interest for me. One such tale is this: it came to me in a place very remote from Seaburgh, and quite accidentally, from a man whom I had been able to oblige—enough in his opinion to justify his making me his confidant to this extent.

I know all that country more or less (he said). I used to go to Scaburgh pretty regularly for golf in the spring. I generally put up at the 'Bear', with a friend—Henry Long it was, you knew him perhaps—('Slightly,' I said) and we used to take a sitting-room and be very happy there. Since he died I haven't cared to go there. And I don't know that I should anyhow after the particular thing that happened on our last visit.
It was in April, 19—, we were there, and by some chance we were almost the only people in the hotel. So the ordinary public rooms were practically empty, and we were the more surprised when, after dinner, our sitting-room door opened,

2

and a young man put his head in. We were aware of this young man. He was rather a rabbity anaemic subject— light hair and light eyes—but not unpleasing. So when he said: 'I beg your pardon, is this a private room?' we did not growl and say: 'Yes, it is,' but Long said, or I did—no matter which: 'Please come in.' 'Oh, may I?' he said, and seemed relieved. Of course it was obvious that he wanted company; and as he was a reasonable kind of person—not the sort to bestow his whole family history on you—we urged him to make himself at home. 'I dare say you find the other rooms rather bleak,' I said. Yes, he did: but it was really too good of us, and so on. That being got over, he made some pretence of reading a book. Long was playing Patience, I was writing. It became plain to me after a few minutes that this visitor of ours was in rather a state of fidgets or nerves, which communicated itself to me, and so I put away my writing and turned to at engaging him in talk.

After some remarks, which I forget, he became rather confidential. 'You'll think it very odd of me' (this was the sort of way he began), 'but the fact is I've had something of a shock.' Well, I recommended a drink of some cheering kind, and we had it. The waiter coming in made an interruption (and I thought our young man seemed very jumpy when the door opened), but after a while he got back to his woes again. There was nobody he knew in the place, and he did happen to know who we both were (it turned out there was some common acquaintance in town), and really he did want a word of advice, if we didn't mind. Of course we both said: 'By all means,' or 'Not at all,' and Long put away his cards. And we settled down to hear what his difficulty was.

'It began,' he said, 'more than a week ago, when I bicycled over to Froston, only about five or six miles, to see the church;

3

I'm very much interested in architecture, and it's got one of those pretty porches with niches and shields. I took a photograph of it, and then an old man who was tidying up in the churchyard came and asked if I'd care to look into the church. I said yes, and he produced a key and let me in. There wasn't much inside, but I told him it was a nice little church, and he kept it very clean, "But," I said, "the porch is the best part of it." We were just outside the porch then, and he said, "Ah, yes, that is a nice porch; and do you know, sir, what's the meanin' of that coat of arms there?"

'It was the one with the three crowns, and though. I'm not much of a herald, I was able to say yes, I thought it was the old arms of the kingdom of East Anglia.

"'That's right, sir," he said, "and do you know the meanin' of them three crowns that's on it?"

'I said I'd no doubt it was known, but I couldn't recollect to have heard it myself.

"'Well, then," he said, "for all you're a scholard, I can tell you something you don't know. Them's the three 'oly crowns what was buried in the ground near by the coast to keep the Germans from landing—ah, I can see you don't believe that. But I tell you, if it hadn't have been for one of them 'oly crowns bein' there still, them Germans would a landed here time and again, they would. Landed with their ships, and killed man, woman and child in their beds. Now then, that's the truth what I'm telling you, that is; and if you don't believe me, you ast the rector. There he comes: you ast him, I says."

'I looked round, and there was the rector, a nice-looking old man, coming up the path; and before I could begin assuring my old man, who was getting quite excited, that I didn't disbelieve him, the rector struck in, and said:

"'What's all this about, John? Good day to you, sir. Have you been looking at our little church?'"

'So then there was a little talk which allowed the old man to calm down, and then the rector asked him again what was the matter.

"'Oh," he said, "it warn't nothink, only I was telling this gentleman he'd ought to ast you about them 'oly crowns."

"'Ah, yes, to be sure," said the rector, "that's a very curious matter, isn't it? But I don't know whether the gentleman is interested in our old stories, eh?"

"'Oh, he'll be interested fast enough," says the old man, "he'll put his confidence in what you tells him, sir; why, you known William Ager yoursell, father and son too."

'Then I put in a word to say how much I should like to hear all about it, and before many minutes I was walking up the village street with the rector, who had one or two words to say to parishioners, and then to the rectory, where he took me into his study. He had made out, on the way, that I really was capable of taking an intelligent interest in a piece of folklore, and not quite the ordinary tripper. So he was very willing to talk, and it is rather surprising to me that the particular legend he told me has not made its way into print before. His account of it was this: "There has always been a belief in these parts in the three holy crowns. The old people say they were buried in different places near the coast to keep off the Danes or the French or the Germans. And they say that one of the

5

three was dug up a long time ago, and another has disappeared by the encroaching of the sea, and one's still left doing its work, keeping off invaders. Well, now, if you have read the ordinary guides and histories of this county, you will remember perhaps that in 1687 a crown, which was said to be the crown of Redwald, King of the East Angles, was dug up at Rendlesham, and alas! alas! melted down before it was even properly described or drawn. Well, Rendlesham isn't on the coast, but it isn't so very far inland, and it's on a very important line of access. And I believe that is the crown which the people mean when they say that one has been dug up. Then on the south you don't want me to tell you where there was a Saxon royal palace which is now under the sea, eh? Well, there was the second crown, I take it. And up beyond these two, they say, lies the third."

'"Do they say where it is?" of course I asked.

'He said, "Yes, indeed, they do, but they don't tell," and his manner did not encourage me to put the obvious question. Instead of that I waited a moment, and said: "What did the old man mean when he said you knew William Ager, as if that had something to do with the crowns?"

'"To be sure," he said, "now that's another curious story. These Agers it's a very old name in these parts, but I can't find that they were ever people of quality or big owners these Agers say, or said, that their branch of the family were the guardians of the last crown. A certain old Nathaniel Ager was the first one I knew—I was born and brought up quite near here—and he, I believe, camped out at the place during the whole of the war of 1870. William, his son, did the same, I know, during the South African War. And young William, his son, who has only died fairly recently, took lodgings at the cottage nearest the spot; and I've no doubt hastened his end,

6

for he was a consumptive, by exposure and night watching. And he was the last of that branch. It was a dreadful grief to him to think that he was the last, but he could do nothing, the only relations at all near to him were in the colonies. I wrote letters for him to them imploring them to come over on business very important to the family, but there has been no answer. So the last of the holy crowns, if it's there, has no guardian now."

'That was what the rector told me, and you can fancy how interesting I found it. The only thing I could think of when I left him was how to hit upon the spot where the crown was supposed to be. I wish I'd left it alone.

'But there was a sort of fate in it, for as I bicycled back past the churchyard wall my eye caught a fairly new gravestone, and on it was the name of William Ager. Of course I got off and read it. It said "of this parish, died at Seaburgh, 19—, aged 28."'There it was, you see. A little judicious questioning in the right place, and I should at least find the cottage nearest the spot. Only I didn't quite know what was the right place to begin my questioning at. Again there was fate: it took me to the curiosity-shop down that way—you know—and I turned over some old books, and, if you please, one was a prayer-book of 1740 odd, in a rather handsome binding—I'll just go and get it, it's in my room.'

He left us in a state of some surprise, but we had hardly time to exchange any remarks when he was back, panting, and handed us the book opened at the fly-leaf, on which was, in a straggly hand:

'Nathaniel Ager is my name and England is my nation,

Seaburgh is my dwelling-place and Christ is my Salvation,
When I am dead and in my Grave, and all my bones are rotton,
I hope the Lord will think on me when I am quite forgotton.'

This poem was dated 1754, and there were many more entries of Agers, Nathaniel, Frederick, William, and so on, ending with William, 19—.

'You see,' he said, 'anybody would call it the greatest bit of luck. I did, but I don't now. Of course I asked the shopman about William Ager, and of course he happened to remember that he lodged in a cottage in the North Field and died there. This was just chalking the road for me. I knew which the cottage must be: there is only one sizable one about there. The next thing was to scrape some sort of acquaintance with the people, and I took a walk that way at once. A dog did the business for me: he made at me so fiercely that they had to run out and beat him off, and then naturally begged my pardon, and we got into talk. I had only to bring up Ager's name, and pretend I knew, or thought I knew something of him, and then the woman said how sad it was him dying so young, and she was sure it came of him spending the night out of doors in the cold weather. Then I had to say: "Did he go out on the sea at night?" and she said: "Oh, no, it was on the hillock yonder with the trees on it." And there I was.

'I know something about digging in these barrows: I've opened many of them in the down country. But that was with owner's leave, and in broad daylight and with men to help. I had to prospect very carefully here before I put a spade in: I couldn't trench across the mound, and with those old firs

8

growing there I knew there would be awkward tree roots. Still the soil was very light and sandy and easy, and there was a rabbit hole or so that might be developed into a sort of tunnel. The going out and coming back at odd hours to the hotel was going to be the awkward part. When I made up my mind about the way to excavate I told the people that I was called away for a night, and I spent it out there. I made my tunnel: I won't bore you with the details of how I supported it and filled it in when I'd done, but the main thing is that I got the crown.'

Naturally we both broke out into exclamations of surprise and interest. I for one had long known about the finding of the crown at Rendlesham and had often lamented its fate. No one has ever seen an Anglo-Saxon crown — at least no one had. But our man gazed at us with a rueful eye. 'Yes,' he said, 'and the worst of it is I don't know how to put it back.'

'Put it back?' we cried out. 'Why, my dear sir, you've made one of the most exciting finds ever heard of in this country. Of course it ought to go to the Jewel Houise at the Tower. What's your difficulty? If you're thinking about the owner of the land, and treasure-trove, and all that, we can certainly help you through. Nobody's going to make a fuss about technicalities in a case of this kind.'

Probably more was said, but all he did was to put his face in his hands, and mutter: 'I don't know how to put it back.'

At last Long said: 'You'll forgive me, I hope, if I seem impertinent, but are you quite sure you've got it?' I was wanting to ask much the same question myself, for of course the story did seem a lunatic's dream when one thought over it. But I hadn't quite dared to say what might hurt the poor young man's feelings. However, he took it quite calmly—really, with the calm of despair, you might say. He sat up and said: 'Oh, yes, there's no doubt of that: I have it here, in my room, locked up in my bag. You can come and look at it if you like: I won't offer to bring it here.'

We were not likely to let the chance slip. We went with him; his room was only a few doors off. The boots was just collecting shoes in the passage: or so we thought: afterwards we were not sure. Our visitor— his name was Parton—was in a worse state of shivers than before, and went hurriedly into the room, and beckoned us after him, turned on the light, and shut the door carefully. Then he unlocked his kit-bag, and produced a bundle of clean pocket-handkerchiefs in which something was wrapped, laid it on the bed, and undid it. I can now say I have seen an actual Anglo-Saxon crown. It was of silver—as the Rendlesham one is always said to have been—it was set with some gems, mostly antique intaglios and cameos, and was of rather plain, almost rough workmanship. In fact, it was like those you see on the coins and in the manuscripts. I found no reason to think it was later than the ninth century. I was intensely interested, of course, and I wanted to turn it over in my hands, but Paxton prevented me. 'Don't you touch it,' he said, 'I'll do that.' And with a sigh that was, I declare to you, dreadful to hear, he took it up and turned it about so that we could see every part of it. 'Seen enough?' he said at last, and we nodded. He wrapped it up and locked it in his bag, and stood looking at us dumbly. 'Come back to our room,' Long said, 'and tell us what the trouble is.' He thanked us, and said: 'Will you go first and see if—if the coast is clear?' That wasn't very intelligible, for our proceedings hadn't been, after all, very suspicious, and the hotel, as I said, was practically empty. However, we were beginning to have inklings of—we didn't

10

know what, and anyhow nerves are infectious. So we did go, first peering out as we opened the door, and fancying (I found we both had the fancy) that a shadow, or more than a shadow—but it made no sound—passed from before us to one side as we came out into the passage. 'It's all right,' we whispered to Paxton—whispering seemed the proper tone— and we went, with him between us, back to our sitting-room. I was preparing, when we got there, to be ecstatic about the unique interest of what we had seen, but when I looked at Paxton I saw that would be terribly out of place, and I left it to him to begin.

'What is to be done?' was his opening. Long thought it right (as he explained to me afterwards) to be obtuse, and said: 'Why not find out who the owner of the land is, and inform—' Oh, no, no!' Paxton broke in impatiently, 'I beg your pardon: you've been very kind, but don't you see it's got to go back, and I daren't be there at night, and daytime's impossible. Perhaps, though, you don't see: well, then, the truth is that I've never been alone since I touched it.' I was beginning some fairly stupid comment, but Long caught my eye, and I stopped. Long said: 'I think I do see, perhaps: but wouldn't it be a relief—to tell us a little more clearly what the situation is?'

Then it all came out: Paxton looked over his shoulder and beckoned to us to come nearer to him, and began speaking in a low voice: we listened most intently, of course, and compared notes afterwards, and I wrote down our version, so I am confident I have what he told us almost word for word. He said: 'It began when I was first prospecting, and put me off again and again. There was always somebody—a man— standing by one of the firs. This was in daylight, you know. He was never in front of me. I always saw him with the tail of

11

my eye on the left or the right, and he was never there when I looked straight for him. I would lie down for quite a long time and take careful observations, and make sure there was no one, and then when I got up and began prospecting again, there he was. And he began to give me hints, besides; for wherever I put that prayer-book—short of locking it up, which I did at last—when I came back to my loom it was always out on my table open at the fly-leaf where the names are, and one of my razors across it to keep it open. I'm sure he just can't open my bag, or something more would have happened. You see, he's light and weak, but all the same I daren't face him. Well, then, when I was making the tunnel, of course it was worse, and if I hadn't been so keen I should have dropped the whole thing and run. It was like someone scraping at my back all the time: I thought for a long time it was only soil dropping on me, but as I got nearer the—the crown, it was unmistakable. And when I actually laid it bare and got my fingers into the ring of it and pulled it out, there came a sort of cry behind me— oh, I can't tell you how desolate it was! And horribly threatening too. It spoilt all my pleasure in my find—cut it off that moment. And if I hadn't been the wretched fool I am, I should have put the thing back and left it. But I didn't. The rest of the time was just awful. I had hours to get through before I could decently come back to the hotel. First I spent time filling up my tunnel and covering my tracks, and all the while he was there trying to thwart me. Sometimes, you know, you see him, and sometimes you don't, just as he pleases, I think: he's there, but he has some power over your eyes. Well, I wasn't off the spot very long before sunrise, and then I had to get to the junction for Seaburgh, and take a train back. And though it was daylight fairly soon, I don't know if that made it much better. There were always hedges, or gorse-bushes, or park fences along the road— some sort of cover, I mean—and I was never easy for a second. And then when I began to meet people going to work, they always looked behind me very strangely: it might have been that they were surprised at seeing anyone so early; but I didn't think it was only that, and I don't now: they didn't look exactly at me. And the porter at the train was like that too. And the guard held open the door after I'd got into the carriage—just as he would if there was somebody else coming, you know. Oh, you may be very sure it isn't my fancy,' he said with a dull sort of laugh. Then he went on: 'And even if I do get it put back, he won't forgive me: I can tell that. And I was so happy a fortnight ago.' He dropped into a chair, and I believe he began to cry.

We didn't know what to say, but we felt we must come to the rescue somehow, and so—it really seemed the only thing—we said if he was so set on putting the crown back in its place, we would help him. And I must say that after what we had heard it did seem the right thing. If these horrid consequences had come on this poor man, might there not really be something in the original idea of the crown having some curious power bound up with it, to guard the coast? At least, that was my feeling, and I think it was Long's too. Our offer was very welcome to Paxton, anyhow. When could we do it? It was nearing half-past ten. Could we contrive to make a late walk plausible to the hotel people that very night? We looked out of the window: there was a brilliant full moon—the Paschal moon. Long undertook to tackle the boots and propitiate him. He was to say that we should not be much over the hour, and if we did find it so pleasant that we stopped out a bit longer we would see that he didn't lose by sitting up. Well, we were pretty regular customers of the hotel, and did not give much trouble, and were considered by the servants to be not under the mark in the way of tips; and so the boots was propitiated, and let us out on to the sea-

13

front, and remained, as we heard later, looking after us. Paxton had a large coat over his arm, under which was the wrapped-up crown.

So we were off on this strange errand before we had time to think how very much out of the way it was. I have told this part quite shortly on purpose, for it really does represent the haste with which we settled our plan and took action. 'The shortest way is up the hill and through the churchyard,' Paxton said, as we stood a moment before, the hotel looking up and down the front. There was nobody about—nobody at all. Seaburgh out of the season is an early, quiet place. 'We can't go along the dyke by the cottage, because of the dog,' Paxton also said, when I pointed to what I thought a shorter way along the front and across two fields. The reason he gave was good enough. We went up the road to the church, and turned in at the churchyard gate. I confess to having thought that there might be some one lying there who might be conscious of our business: but if it was so, they were also conscious that one who was on their side, so to say, had us under surveillance, and we saw no sign of them. But under observation we felt we were, as I have never felt it at another time. Specially was it so when we passed out of the churchyard into a narrow path with close high hedges, through which we hurried as Christian did through that Valley; and so got out into open fields. Then along hedges, though I world sooner have been in the open, where I could see if anyone was visible behind me; over a gate or two, and then a swerve to the left, taking us up on to the ridge which ended in that mound.

As we neared it, Henry Long felt, and I felt too, that there were what I can only call dim presences waiting for us, as well as a far more actual one attending us. Of Paxton's agitation all this time I can give you no adequate picture: he breathed like a hunted beast, and we could not either of us look at his face. How he would manage when we got to the very place we had not troubled to think: he had seemed so sure that that would not be difficult. Nor was it. I never saw anything like the dash with which he flung himself at a particular spot in the side of the mound, and tore at it, so that in a very few minutes the greater part of his body was out of sight. We stood holding the coat and that bundle of handkerchiefs, and looking, very fearfully, I must admit, about us. There was nothing to be seen: a line of dark firs behind us made one skyline, more trees and the church tower half a mile off on the right, cottages and a windmill on the horizon on the left, calm sea dead in front, faint barking of a dog at a cottage on a gleaming dyke between us and it: full moon making that path we know across the sea: the eternal whisper of the Scotch firs just above us, and of the sea in front. Yet, in all this quiet, an acute, an acrid consciousness of a restrained hostility very near us, like a dog on a leash that might be let go at any moment.

Paxton pulled himself out of the hole, and stretched a hand back to us. 'Give it to me,' he whispered, 'unwrapped.' We pulled off the handkerchiefs, and he took the crown. The moonlight just fell on it as he snatched it. We had not ourselves touched that bit of metal, and I have thought since that it was just as well. In another moment Paxton was out of the hole again and busy shovelling back the soil with hands that were already bleeding He would have none of our help though It was much the longest part of the job to get the place to look undisturbed yet—I don't know how—he made a wonderful success of it. At last he was satisfied and we turned back.

We were a couple of hundred yards from the hill when Long suddenly said to him: 'I say you've left your coat there. That won't do. See?' And I certainly did see it—the long dark overcoat lying where the tunnel had been. Paxton had not stopped, however: he only shook his head, and held up the coat on his arm. And when we joined him, he said, without any excitement, but as if nothing mattered any more: 'That wasn't my coat.' And, indeed, when we looked back again, that dark thing was not to be seen.

Well, we got out on to the road, and came rapidly back that way. It was well before twelve when we got in, trying to put a good face on it, and saying—Long and I—what a lovely night it was for a walk. The boots was on the look-out for us, and we made remarks like that for his edification as we entered the hotel. He gave another look up and down the sea-front before he locked the front door, and said: 'You didn't meet many people about, I s'pose, sir?' 'No, indeed, not a soul,' I said; at which I remember Paxton looked oddly at me. 'Only I thought I see someone turn up the station road after you gentlemen,' said the boots. 'Still, you was three together, and I don't suppose he meant mischief.' I didn't know what to say; Long merely said 'Good night,' and we went off upstairs, promising to turn out all lights, and to go to bed in a few minutes.

Back in our room, we did our very best to make Paxton take a cheerful view. There's the crown safe back,' we said; 'very likely you'd have done better not to touch it' (and he heavily assented to that), 'but no real harm has been done, and we shall never give this away to anyone who would be so mad as to go near it. Besides, don't you feel better yourself? I don't mind confessing,' I said, 'that on the way there I was very much inclined to take your view about—well, about being

16

followed; but going back, it wasn't at all the same thing, was it?' No, it wouldn't do: 'You've nothing to trouble yourselves about,' he said, 'but I'm not forgiven. I've got to pay for that miserable sacrilege still. I know what you are going to say. The Church might help. Yes, but it's the body that has to suffer. It's true I'm not feeling that he's waiting outside for me just now. But—' Then he stopped. Then he turned to thanking us, and we put him off as soon as we could. And naturally we pressed him to use our sitting-room next day, and said we should be glad to go out with him. Or did he play golf, perhaps? Yes, he did, but he didn't think he should care about that tomorrow. Well, we recommended him to get up late and sit in our room in the morning while we were playing, and we would have a walk later in the day. He was very submissive and piano about it all: ready to do just what we thought best, but clearly quite certain in his own mind that what was coming could not be averted or palliated. You'll wonder why we didn't insist on accompanying him to his home and seeing him safe into the care of brothers or someone. The fact was he had nobody. He had had a flat in town, but lately he had made up his mind to settle for a time in Sweden, and he had dismantled his flat and shipped off his belongings, and was whiling away a fortnight or three weeks before he made a start. Anyhow, we didn't see what we could do better than sleep on it—or not sleep very much, as was my case and see what we felt like tomorrow morning.

We felt very different, Long and I, on as beautiful an April morning as you could desire; and Paxton also looked very different when we saw him at breakfast. 'The first approach to a decent night I seem ever to have had,' was what he said. But he was going to do as we had settled: stay in probably all the morning, and come out with us later. We went to the links; we met some other men and played with them in the morning, and had lunch there rather early, so as not to be late back. All the same, the snares of death overtook him.

Whether it could have been prevented, I don't know. I think he would have been got at somehow, do what we might. Anyhow, this is what happened.

We went straight up to our room. Paxton was there, reading quite peaceably. 'Ready to come out shortly?' said Long, 'say in half an hour's time?' 'Certainly,' he said: and I said we would change first, and perhaps have baths, and call for him in half an hour. I had my bath first, and went and lay down on my bed, and slept for about ten minutes. We came out of our rooms at the same time, and went together to the sitting-room. Paxton wasn't there—only his book. Nor was he in his room, nor in the downstair rooms. We shouted for him. A servant came out and said: 'Why, I thought you gentlemen was gone out already, and so did the other gentleman. He heard you a-calling from the path there, and run out in a hurry, and I looked out of the coffee-room window, but I didn't see you. 'Owever, he run off down the beach that way.'

Without a word we ran that way too—it was the opposite direction to that of last night's expedition. It wasn't quite four o'clock, and the day was fair, though not so fair as it had been, so that was really no reason, you'd say, for anxiety: with people about, surely a man couldn't come to much harm.

But something in our look as we ran out must have struck the servant, for she came out on the steps, and pointed, and said, 'Yes, that's the way he went.' We ran on as far as the top of the shingle bank, and there pulled up. There was a choice of ways: past the houses on the sea-front, or along the sand at the bottom of the beach, which, the tide being now out, was fairly broad. Or of course we might keep along the shingle between these two tracks and have some view of both of them; only that was heavy going. We chose the sand, for that was the loneliest, and someone might come to harm there without being seen from the public path.

Long said he saw Paxton some distance ahead, running and waving his stick, as if he wanted to signal to people who were on ahead of him. I couldn't be sure: one of these sea-mists was coming up very quickly from the south. There was someone, that's all I could say. And there were tracks on the sand as of someone running who wore shoes; and there were other tracks made before those—for the shoes sometimes trod in them and interfered with them—of someone not in shoes. Oh, of course, it's only my word you've got to take for all this: Long's dead, we'd no time or means to make sketches or take casts, and the next tide washed everything away. All we could do was to notice these marks as we hurried on. But there they were over and over again, and we had no doubt whatever that what we saw was the track of a bare foot, and one that showed more bones than flesh.

The notion of Paxton running after—after anything like this, and supposing it to be the friends he was looking for, was very dreadful to us. You can guess what we fancied: how the thing he was following might stop suddenly and turn round on him, and what sort of face it would show, half-seen at first in the mist—which all the while was getting thicker and thicker. And as I ran on wondering how the poor wretch could have been lured into mistaking that other thing for us, I remembered his saying, 'He has some power over your eyes.' And then I wondered what the end would be, for I had no hope now that the end could be averted, and—well, there is no need to tell all the dismal and horrid thoughts that flitted through my head as we ran on into the mist. It was uncanny,

19

too, that the sun should still be bright in the sky and we could see nothing. We could only tell that we were now past the houses and had reached that gap there is between them and the old martello tower. When you are past the tower, you know, there is nothing but shingle for a long way—not a house, not a human creature; just that spit of land, or rather shingle, with the river on your right and the sea on your left.

But just before that, just by the martello tower, you remember there is the old battery, close to the sea. I believe there are only a few blocks of concrete left now: the rest has all been washed away, but at this time there was a lot more, though the place was a ruin. Well, when we got there, we clambered to the top as quick as we could to take breath and look over the shingle in front if by chance the mist would let us see anything. But a moment's rest we must have. We had run a mile at least. Nothing whatever was visible ahead of us, and we were just turning by common consent to get down and run hopelessly on, when we heard what I can only call a laugh: and if you can understand what I mean by a breathless, a lungless laugh, you have it: but I don't suppose you can. It came from below, and swerved away into the mist. That was enough. We bent over the wall. Paxton was there at the bottom.

You don't need to be told that he was dead. His tracks showed that he had run along the side of the battery, had turned sharp round the corner of it, and, small doubt of it, must have dashed straight irito the open arms of someone who was waiting there. His mouth was full of sand and stones, and his teeth and jaws were broken to bits. I only glanced once at his face.

At the same moment, just as we were scrambling down from

the battery to get to the body, we heard a shout, and saw a man running down the bank of the martello tower. He was the caretaker stationed there, and his keen old eyes had managed to descry through the mist that something was wrong. He had seen Paxton fall, and had seen us a moment after, running up—fortunate this, for otherwise we could hardly have escaped suspicion of being concerned in the dreadful business. Had he, we asked, caught sight of anybody attacking our friend? He could not be sure.

We sent him off for help, and stayed by the dead man till they came with the stretcher. It was then that we traced out how he had come, on the narrow fringe of sand under the battery wall. The rest was shingle, and it was hopelessly impossible to tell whither the other had gone.

What were we to say at the inquest? It was a duty, we felt, not to give up, there and then, the secret of the crown, to be published in every paper. I don't know how much you would have told; but what we did agree upon was this: to say that we had only made acquaintance with Paxton the day before, and that he had told us he was under some apprehension of danger at the hands of a man called William Ager. Also that we had seen some other tracks besides Paxton's when we followed him along the beach. But of course by that time everything was gone from the sands.

No one had any knowledge, fortunately, of any William Ager living in the district. The evidence of the man at the martello tower freed us from all suspicion. All that could be done was to return a verdict of wilful murder by some person or persons unknowtn.

Paxton was so totally without connections that all the

inquiries that were subsequently made ended in a No Thoroughfare. And I have never been at Seaburgh, or even near it, since.

# THE UNCOMMON PRAYER – BOOK

Mr Davidson was spending the first week in January alone in a country town. A combination of circumstances had driven him to that drastic course: his nearest relations were enjoying winter sports abroad, and the friends who had been kindly anxious to replace them had an infectious complaint in the house. Doubtless he might have found someone else to take pity on him; 'but,' he reflected, 'most of them have made up their parties, and after all it is only for three or four days at most that I have to fend for myself, and it will be just as well if I can get a move on with my introduction to the Leventhorp Papers. I might use the time by going down as near as I can to Gaulsford and making acquaintance with the neighbourhood. I ought to see the remains of the Leventhorp house, and the tombs in the church.'

The first day after his arrival at the Swan Hotel at Longbridge was so stormy that he got no farther than the tobacconist's. The next, comparatively bright, he used for his visit to Gaulsford, which interested him more than a little, but had no ulterior consequences. The third, which was really a pearl of a day for early January, was too fine to be spent indoors. He gathered from the landlord that a favourite practice of visitors in the summer was to take a morning train to a couple of stations westward and walk back down the valley of the Tent, through Stanford St Thomas and Stanford Magdalene, both of which were accounted highly picturesque villages. He closed with this plan, and we now find him seated in a third-class carriage at 9.45 a.m., on his way to Kingsbourne Junction, and studying the map of the district.

One old man was his only fellow-traveller, a piping old man, who seemed inclined for conversation. So Mr Davidson, after going through the necessary versicles and responses about the weather, inquired whether he was going far.

'No, sir, not far, not this morning, sir,' said the old man. 'I ain't only goin' so far as what they call Kingsbourne Junction. There isn't but two stations betwixt here and there. Yes, they calls it Kingsbourne Junction.'

'I'm going there, too,' said Mr Davidson.

'Oh indeed, sir! do you know that part?'

'No, I'm only going for the sake of taking a walk back to Longbridge, and seeing a bit of the country.'

'Oh indeed, sir! Well, 'tis a beautiful day for a gentleman as enjoys a bit of a walk.'

'Yes, to be sure. Have you got far to go when you get to Kingsbourne?'

'No, sir, I ain't got far to go, once I get to Kingsbourne Junction. I'm agoin' to see my daughter, sir. She live at Brockstone. That's about two mile across the fields from what they call Kingsbourne Junction, that is. You've got that marked down on your map, I expect, sir.'

'I expect I have. Let me see, Brockstone, did you say? Here's Kingsbourne, yes; and which way is Brockstone toward the

Stanfords? Ah, I see it: Brockstone Court, in a park. I don't see the village, though.'

'No, sir, you wouldn't see no village of Brockstone. There ain't only the Court and the chapel at Brockstone.'

'Chapel? Oh yes, that's marked here too. The chapel; close by the Court, it seems to be. Does it belong to the Court?'

'Yes, sir, that's close up to the Court, only a step. Yes, that belong to the Court. My daughter, you see, sir, she's the keeper's wife now, and she live at the Court and look after things now the family's away.'

'No one living there now, then?'

'No, sir, not for a number of years. The old gentleman he lived there when I was a lad, and the lady she lived on after him to very near upon ninety years of age. And then she died, and them that have it now, they've got this other place, in Warwickshire I believe it is, and they don't do nothin' about lettin' the Court out; but Colonel Wildman he have the shooting, and young Mr Clark, he's the agent, he come over once in so many weeks to see to things, and my daughter's husband he's the keeper.'

'And who uses the chapel? just the people round about, I suppose.'

'Oh no, no one don't use the chapel. Why, there ain't no one to go. All the people about, they go to Stanford St Thomas Church; but my son-in-law he go to Kingsbourne Church now, because the gentleman at Stanford he have this Gregory singin', and my son-in-law he don't like that; he say he can hear the old donkey brayin' any day of the week, and he like something a little cheerful on the Sunday.' The old man drew his hand across his mouth and laughed. 'That's what my son-in-law say: he say he can hear the old donkey [etc., do copo].'

Mr Davidson also laughed as honestly as he could, thinking meanwhile that Brockstone Court and chapel would probably be worth including in his walk, for the map showed that from Brockstone he could strike the Tent Valley quite as easily as by following the main Kingsbourne-Longbridge road. So, when the mirth excited by the remembrance of the son-in-law's bon mot had died down, he returned to the charge, and ascertained that both the Court and the chapel were of the class known as 'old-fashioned places', and that the old man would be very willing to take him thither, and his daughter would be happy to show him whatever she could.

'But that ain't a lot, sir, not as if the family was livin' there; all the lookin'-glasses is covered up, and the paintin's, and the curtains and carpets folded away: not but what I dare say she could show you a pair just to look at, because she go over them to see as the morth shouldn't get into 'em.'

'I shan't mind about that, thank you: if she can show me the inside of the chapel, that's what I'd like best to see.'

'Oh, she can show you that right enough, sir. She have the key of the door, you see, and most weeks she go in and dust about. That's a nice chapel, that is. My son-in-law he say he'll be bound they didn't have none of this Gregory singin' there. Dear! I can't help but smile when I think of him sayin' that about th' old donkey. "I can hear him bray," he say, "any day of the week"; and so he can, sir, that's true, anyway.'

The walk across the fields from Kingsbourne to Brockstone was very pleasant. It lay for the most part on the top of the country, and commanded wide views over a succession of ridges, plough and pasture, or covered with dark-blue woods—all ending, more or less abruptly, on the right, in headlands that overlooked the wide valley of a great western river. The last field they crossed was bounded by a close copse, and no sooner were they in it than the path turned downwards very sharply, and it became evident that Brockstone was neatly fitted into a sudden and very narrow valley. It was not long before they had glimpses of groups of smokeless stone chimneys, and stone-tiled roofs, close beneath their feet; and not many minutes after that, they were wiping their shoes at the back door of Brockstone Court, while the keeper's dogs barked very loudly in unseen places, and Mrs Porter in quick succession screamed at them to be quiet, greeted her father, and begged both her visitors to step in.

It was not to be expected that Mr Davidson should escape being taken through the principal rooms of the Court, in spite of the fact that the house was entirely out of commission. Pictures, carpets, curtains, furniture, were all covered up or put away, as old Mr Avery had said, and the admiration which our friend was very ready to bestow had to be lavished on the proportions of the rooms, and on the one painted ceiling, upon which an artist who had fled from London in the Plague-year had depicted the Triumph of Loyalty and Defeat of Sedition. In this Mr Davidson could show an unfeigned interest. The portraits of Cromwell, Ireton, Bradshaw, Peters, and the rest, writhing in carefully-devised torments, were evidently the part of the design to which most pains had been devoted.

'That were the old Lady Sadleir had that paintin' done, same as the one what put up the chapel. They say she were the first that went up to London to dance on Oliver Cromwell's grave.' So said Mr Avery, and continued musingly: 'Well, I suppose she got some satisfaction to 'er mind, but I don't know as I should want to pay the fare to London and back just for that, and my son-in-law he say the same: he say he don't know as he should have cared to pay all that money only for that. I was tellin' the gentleman as we come along in the train, Mary, what your 'Arry says about this Gregory singin' down at Stanford here. We 'ad a bit of a laugh over that, sir, didn't us?'

'Yes, to be sure we did; ha! ha!' Once again Mr Davidson strove to do justice to the pleasantry of the keeper. 'But,' he said, 'if Mrs Porter can show me the chapel, I think it should be now, for the days aren't long, and I want to get back to Longbridge before it falls quite dark.'

Even if Brockstone Court has not been illustrated in Rural Life (and I think it has not) I do not propose to point out its excellences here; but of the chapel a word must be said. It stands about a hundred yards from the house, and has its own little graveyard and trees about it. It is a stone building about seventy feet long, and in the gothic style, as that style was understood in the middle of the seventeenth century. On the whole it resembles some of the Oxford college chapels as much as anything, save that it has a distinct chancel, like a parish church, and a fanciful domed bell-turret at the south-west angle.

When the west door was thrown open, Mr Davidson could not repress an exclamation of pleased surprise at the completeness and richness of the interior. Screen-work, pulpit, seating, and glass—all were of the same period; and as he advanced into the nave and sighted the organ-case with its gold embossed pipes in the western gallery, his cup of satisfaction was filled. The glass in the nave windows was chiefly armorial; in the chancel were figure-subjects, of the kind that may be seen at Abbey Dore, of Lord Scudamore's work. But this is not an archaeological review.

While Mr Davidson was still busy examining the remains of the organ (attributed to one of the Dallams, I believe) old Mr Avery had stumped up into the chancel and was lifting the dust-cloths from the blue velvet cushions of the stall-desks— evidently it was here that the family sat. Mr Davidson heard him say in a rather hushed tone of surprise, 'Why, Mary, here's all the books open agin!'

The reply was in a voice that sounded peevish rather than surprised. 'Tt-tt-tt, well, there, I never!'

Mrs Porter went over to where her father was standing, and they continued talking in a lower key. Mr Davidson saw plainly that something not quite in the common run was under discussion: so he came down the gallery stairs and joined them. There was no sign of disorder in the chancel any more than in the rest of the chapel, which was beautifully clean, but the eight folio Prayer-Books on the cushions of the stall-desks were indubitably open.

Mrs Porter was inclined to be fretful over it. 'Whoever can it be as does it?' she said, 'for there's no key but mine, nor yet door but the one we come in by, and the winders is barred, every one of 'em: I don't like it, father, that I don't.'

'What is it, Mrs Porter? Anything wrong?' said Mr Davidson.

'No, sir, nothing reely wrong, only these books. Every time pretty near that I come in to do up the place, I shuts 'em and spreads the cloths over 'em to keep off the dust, ever since Mr Clark spoke about it when I first come; and yet there they are again, and always the same page—and as I says, whoever it can be as does it with the door and winders shut; and as I says, it makes anyone feel queer comin' in here alone as I 'ave to do, not as I'm given that way myself, not to be frightened easy, I mean to say; and there's not a rat in the place—not as no rat wouldn't trouble to do a thing like that, do you think, sir?'

'Hardly, I should say; but it sounds very queer. Are they always open at the same place, did you say?'

'Always the same place, sir, one of the psalms it is, and I didn't particular notice it the first time or two, till I see a little red line of printing, and it's always caught my eye since.'

Mr Davidson walked along the stalls and looked at the open books. Sure enough, they all stood at the same page: Psalm cix, and at the head of it, just between the number and the Dens Iaudem, was a rubric, 'For the 25th day of April'. Without pretending to minute knowledge of the history of the Book of Common Prayer, he knew enough to be sure that this was a very odd and wholly unauthorized addition to its text; and though he remembered that April is St Mark's Day, he could not imagine what appropriateness this very savage psalm could have to that festival. With slight misgivings, he ventured to turn over the leaves to examine the title-page, and knowing the need for particular accuracy in these matters, he devoted some ten minutes to making a line-for-line transcript of it. The date was 1653; the printer called himself Anthony Cadman. He turned to the list of Proper

Psalms for certain days: yes, added to it was that same inexplicable entry: For the 25th day of April: the moth Psalm. An expert would no doubt have thought of many other points to inquire into, but this antiquary, as I have said, was no expert. He took stock, however, of the binding, a handsome one of tooled blue leather, bearing the arms that figured in several of the nave windows in various combinations.

'How often,' he said at last to Mrs Porter, 'have you found these books lying open like this?'

'Reely I couldn't say, sir, but it's a great many times now. Do you recollect, father, me telling you about it the first time I noticed it?'
'That I do, my dear: you was in a rare taking, and I don't so much wonder at it; that was five year ago I was paying you a visit at Michaelmas time, and you come in at tea-time, and says you, "Father, there's the books layin' open under the cloths agin"; and I didn't know what my daughter was speakin' about, you see, sir, and I says, "Books?" just like that, I says; and then it all came out. But as Harry says, — that's my son-in-law, sir, — "whoever it can be," he says, "as does it, because there ain't only the one door, and we keeps the key locked up," he says, "and the winders is barred, every one on 'em. Well," he says, "I lay once I could catch 'em at it they wouldn't do it a second time," he says. And no more they wouldn't, I don't believe, sir. Well that was five year ago, and it's been happenin' constant ever since by your account, my dear. Young Mr Clark he don't seem to think much to it, but then he don't live here, you see, and 'tisn't his business to come and clean up here of a dark afternoon, is it?'

'I suppose you never notice anything else odd when you are at work here, Mrs Porter?' said Mr Davidson.

'No, sir, I do not,' said Mrs Porter, 'and it's a funny thing to me I don't, with the feeling I have as there's someone settin' here—no, it's the other side, just within the screen—and lookin' at me all the time I'm dustin' in the gallery and pews. But I never yet see nothin' worse than myself, as the sayin' goes, and I kindly hope I never may.'

In the conversation that followed (there was not much of it) nothing was added to the statement of the case. Having parted on good terms with Mr Avery and his daughter, Mr Davidson addressed himself to his eight-mile walk. The little valley of Brockstone soon led him down into the broader one of the Tent, and on to Stanford St Thomas, where he found refreshment.

We need not accompany him all the way to Longbridge. But as he was changing his socks before dinner, he suddenly paused and said half-aloud, 'By Jove, that is a rum thing!' It had not occurred to him before how strange it was that any edition of the Prayer-Book should have been issued in 1653, seven years before the Restoration, five years before Cromwell's death, and when the use of the book, let alone the printing of it, was penal. He must have been a bold man who put his name and a date on that title-page. Only, Mr Davidson reflected, it probably was not his name at all, for the ways of printers in difficult times were devious.

As he was in the front hall of the Swan that evening, making some investigations about trains, a small motor stopped in front of the door, and out of it came a small man in a fur coat, who stood on the steps and gave directions in a rather yapping foreign accent to his chauffeur. When he came into the hotel, he was seen to be black-haired and pale-faced, with a little pointed beard, and gold pince-nez; altogether, very neatly turned out.

He went to his room, and Mr Davidson saw no more of him till dinner-time. As they were the only two dining that night, it was not difficult for the newcomer to find an excuse for falling into talk; he was evidently wishing to make out what brought Mr Davidson into that neighbourhood at that season.

'Can you tell me how far it is from here to Arlingworth?' was one of his early questions, and it was one which threw some light on his own plans, for Mr Davidson recollected having seen at the station an advertisement of a sale at Arlingworth Hall, comprising old furniture, pictures, and books. This, then, was a London dealer.

'No,' he said, 'I've never been there. I believe it lies out by Kingsbourne—it can't be less than twelve miles. I see there's a sale there shortly.'

The other looked at him inquisitively, and he laughed. 'No,' he said, as if answering a question, 'you needn't be afraid of my competing; I'm leaving this place tomorrow.'

This cleared the air, and the dealer, whose name was Homberger, admitted that he was interested in books, and thought there might be in these old country-house libraries something to repay a journey. 'For,' said he, 'we English have always this marvellous talent for accumulating rarities in the most unexpected places, ain't it?'

And in the course of the evening he was most interesting on the subject of finds made by himself and others. 'I shall take the occasion after this sale to look round the district a bit:

perhaps you could inform me of some likely spots, Mr Davidson?' But Davidson, though he had seen some very tempting locked-up bookcases at Brockstone Court, kept his counsel. He did not really like Mr Homberger.

Next day, as he sat in the train, a little ray of light came to illuminate one of yesterday's puzzles. He happened to take out an almanac-diary that he had bought for the new year, and it occurred to him to look at the remarkable events for April 25. There it was: 'St Mark. Oliver Cromwell born, 1599.'

That, coupled with the painted ceiling, seemed to explain a good deal. The figure of old Lady Sadleir became more substantial to his imagination, as of one in whom love for Church and King had gradually given place to intense hate of the power that had silenced the one and slaughtered the other. What curious evil service was that which she and a few like her had been wont to celebrate year by year in that remote valley? and how in the world had she managed to elude authority? And again, did not this persistent opening of the books agree oddly with the other traits of her portrait known to him?

It would be interesting for anyone who chanced to be near Brockstone on the twenty-fifth of April to look in at the chapel and see if anything exceptional happened. When he came to think of it, there seemed to be no reason why he should not be that person himself: he, and if possible, some congenial friend. He resolved that so it should be.

Knowing that he knew really nothing about the printing of Prayer-Books, he realized that he must make it his business to get the best light on the matter without divulging his reasons. I may say at once that his search was entirely fruitless. One writer of the early part of the nineteenth century, a writer of rather windy and rhapsodical chat about books, professed to have heard of a special anti-Cromwellian issue of the Prayer-Book in the very midst of the Commonwealth period. But he did not claim to have seen a copy, and no one had believed him. Looking into this matter, Mr Davidson found that the statement was based on letters from a correspondent who had lived near Longbridge: so he was inclined to think that the Brockstone Prayer-Books were at the bottom of it, and had excited a momentary interest.

Months went on, and St Mark's Day came near. Nothing interfered with Mr Davidson's plans of visiting Brockstone, or with those of the friend whom he had persuaded to go with him, and to whom alone he had confided the puzzle. The same 9.45 train which had taken him in January took them now to Kingsbourne; the same field-path led them to Brockstone. But today they stopped more than once to pick a cowslip; the distant woods and ploughed uplands were of another colour, and in the copse there was, as Mrs Porter said, 'a regular charm of birds; why you couldn't hardly collect your mind sometimes with it.'

She recognized Mr Davidson at once and was very ready to do the honours of the chapel. The new visitor, Mr Witham, was as much struck by the completeness of it as Mr Davidson had been. 'There can't be such another in England,' he said.

'Books open again, Mrs Porter?' said Davidson, as they walked up to the chancel.

'Dear, yes, I expect so, sir,' said Mrs Porter, as she drew off the cloths. 'Well, there!' she exclaimed the next moment, 'if they ain't shut! That's the first time ever I've found 'em so. But it's not for want of care on my part, I do assure you, gentlemen, if they wasn't, for I felt the cloths the last thing before I shut up last week, when the gentleman had done photografting the heast winder, and every one was shut, and where there was ribbons left I tied 'em. Now I think of it, I don't remember ever to 'ave done that before, and per'aps, whoever it is it just made the difference to 'em. Well, it only shows, don't it? If at first you don't succeed, try, try, try again.'

Meanwhile the two men had been examining the books, and now Davidson spoke.

'I'm sorry to say I'm afraid there's something wrong here, Mrs Porter. These are not the same books.'

It would make too long a business to detail all Mrs Porter's outcries, and the questionings that followed. The upshot was this. Early in January the gentleman had come to see over the chapel and thought a great deal of it and said he must come back in the spring weather and take some photografts. And only a week ago he had drove up in his motoring car, and a very 'eavy box with the slides in it, and she had locked him in because he said something about a long explosion, and she was afraid of some damage happening: and he says, no, not explosion, but it appeared the lantern what they take the slides with worked very slow, and so he was in there the best part of an hour and she come and let him out, and he drove off with his box and all and gave her his visiting-card, and oh, dear, dear, to think of such a thing! he must have changed the books and took the old ones away with him in his box.

'What sort of man was he?'

'Oh, dear, he was a small-made gentleman, if you can call him

36

so after the way he've behaved, with black hair, that is if it was hair, and gold eye-glasses, if they was gold: reely, one don't know what to believe. Sometimes I doubt he weren't a reel Englishman at all, and yet he seemed to know the language, and had the name on his visiting-card like anybody else might.

'Just so; might we see the card? Yes: T. W. Henderson, and an address somewhere near Bristol. Well, Mrs Porter, it's quite plain this Mr Henderson, as he calls himself, has walked off with your eight Prayer-Books and put eight others about the same size in place of them. Now listen to me. I suppose you must tell your husband about this, but neither you nor he must say one word about it to anyone else. If you'll give me the address of the agent—Mr Clark, isn't it?—I will write to him and tell him exactly what has happened, and that it really is no fault of yours. But, you understand, we must keep it very quiet: and why? Because this man who has stolen the books will of course try to sell them one at a time—for I may tell you they are worth a good deal of money—and the only way we can bring it home to him is by keeping a sharp look out and saying nothing.'

By dint of repeating the same advice in various forms they succeeded in impressing Mrs Porter with the real need for silence, and were forced to make a concession only in the case of Mr Avery, who was expected on a visit shortly: 'But you may be safe with father, sir,' said Mrs Porter. 'Father ain't a talkin' man.'

It was not quite Mr Davidson's experience of him; still, there were no neighbours at Brockstone, and even Mr Avery must be aware that gossip with anybody on such a subject would

37

be likely to end in the Porters having to look out for another situation.

A last question was whether Mr Henderson, so-called, had anyone with him.

'No, sir, not when he come he hadn't: he was working his own motoring car himself, and what luggage he had, let me see: there was his lantern and this box of slides inside the carriage, which I helped him into the chapel and out of it myself with it, if only I'd knowed! And as he drove away under the big yew tree by the monument I see the long white bundle laying on the top of the coach, what I didn't notice when he drove up. But he set in front, sir, and only the boxes inside behind him. And do you reely think, sir, as his name weren't Henderson at all? Oh dear me, what a dreadful thing! Why fancy what trouble it might bring to a innocent person that might never have set foot in the place but for that!'

They left Mrs Porter in tears. On the way home there was much discussion as to the best means of keeping watch upon possible sales. What Henderson-Homberger (for there could be no real doubt of the identity) had done was, obviously, to bring down the requisite number of folio Prayer-Books— disused copies from college chapels and the like, bought ostensibly for the sake of the bindings, which were superficially like enough to the old ones—and to substitute them at his leisure for the genuine articles. A week had now passed without any public notice being taken of the theft. He would take a little time himself to find out about the rarity of the books, and would ultimately, no doubt, 'place' them cautiously. Between them, Davidson and Witham were in a position to know a good deal of what was passing in the book-world, and they could map out the ground pretty completely. A weak point with them at the moment was that neither of them knew under what other name or names Henderson-Homberger carried on business. But there are ways of solving these problems.

And yet all this planning proved unnecessary.

* * *

We are transported to a London office on this same 25th of April. We find there, within closed doors, late in the day, two police inspectors, a commissionaire, and a youthful clerk. The two latter, both rather pale and agitated in appearance, are sitting on chairs and being questioned.

'How long do you say you've been in this Mr Poschwitz's employment? Six months? And what was his business? Attended sales in various parts and brought home parcels of books. Did he keep a shop anywhere? No? Disposed of 'em here and there, and sometimes to private collectors. Right. Now then, when did he go out last? Rather better than a week ago. Tell you where he was going? No? Said he was going to start next day from his private residence, and shouldn't be at the office—that's here, eh?—before two days: you was to attend as usual. Where is his private residence? Oh, that's the address, Norwood way; I see. Any family? Not in this country? Now, then, what account do you give of what's happened since he came back? Came back on the Tuesday, did he? and this is the Saturday. Bring any books? One package: where is it? In the safe: you got the key? No, to be sure, it's open, of course. How did he seem when he got back—cheerful? Well, but how do you mean curious? Thought he might be in for an illness: he said that, did he? Odd smell got in his nose, couldn't get rid of it: told you to let

39

him know who wanted to see him before you let 'em in? That wasn't usual with him? Much the same all Wednesday, Thursday, Friday. Out a good deal; said he was going to the British Museum. Often went there to make inquiries in the way of his business. Walked up and down a lot in the office when he was in? Anyone call in on those days? Mostly when he was out. Anyone find him in? Oh, Mr Collinson? Who's Mr Collinson? An old customer: know his address? All right, give it us afterwards. Well, now, what about this morning? You left Mr Poschwitz's here at twelve and went home. Anybody see you? Commissionaire, you did? Remained at home till summoned here. Very well.

'Now commissionaire; we have your name—Watkins. eh? Very well, make your statement: don't go too quick, so as we can get it down.'

'I was on duty 'ere later than usual, Mr Potwitch 'axing asked me to remain on, and ordered his lunching to be sent in, which come as ordered. I was in the lobby from eleven-thirty on, and see Mr Bligh [the clerk] leave at about twelve. After that no one come in at all except Mr Potwitch's lunching come at one o'clock and the man left in five minutes' time. Towards the afternoon I became tired of waitin' and I come upstairs to this first floor. The outer door what lead to the orfice stood open, and I come up to the plate-glass door here. Mr Potwitch he was standing behind the table smoking a cigar, and he laid it down on the mantelpiece and felt in his trouser pockets and took out a key and went across to the safe. And I knocked on the glass, thinkin' to see if he wanted me to come and take away his tray, but he didn't take no notice, bein' engaged with the safe door. Then he got it open and stooped down and seemed to be lifting up a package off of the floor of the safe. And then, sir, I see what looked to be like a great roll of old

40

shabby white flannel about four to five feet high fall for'ards out of the inside of the safe right against Mr Potwitch's shoulder as he was stooping over: and Mr Porwitch he raised himself up as it were, resting his hands on the package, and give a exclamation. And I can't hardly expect you should take what I says, but as true as I stand here I see this roll had a kind of a face in the upper end of it, sir. You can't be more surprised than what I was, I can assure you, and I've seen a lot in me time...Yes, I can describe it if you wish it, sir: it was very much the same as this wall here in colour [the wall had an earth-coloured distemper] and it had a bit of a band tied round underneath, and the eyes, well they was dry-like, and much as if there was two big spiders' bodies in the holes...Hair? no, I don't know as there was much hair to be seen: the flannel-stuff was over the top of the 'ead...I'm very sure it warn' t what it should have been. No, I only see it in a flash, but I took it in like a photograft—wish I hadn't...Yest, sir, it fell right over on to Mr Potwitch's shoulder, and this face hid in his neck—yes, sir, about where the injury was— more like a ferret goin' for a rabbit than anythink else, and he rolled over, and of course I tried to get in at the door, but as you know, sir, it were locked on the inside, and all I could do, I rung up everyone, and the surgeon come, and the police and you gentlemen, and you know as much as what I do. If you won't be requirin' me any more today I'd be glad to be gettin' off home: it's shook me up more than I thought for.'

'Well.' said one of the inspectors, when they were left alone, and 'Well?' said the other inspector: and, after a pause, 'What's the surgeon's report again? You've got it there. Yes. Effect on the blood like the worst kind of snake-bite: death almost instantaneous. I'm glad of that for his sake; he was a nasty sight. No case for detaining this man Watkins, anyway; we know all about him. And what about this safe, now? We'd

41

better go over it again, and, by the way, we haven't opened that package he was busy with when he died.'

'Well, handle it careful,' said the other. 'There might be this snake in it, for what you know. Get a light into the corners of the place, too. Well: there's room for a shortish person to stand up in; but what about ventilation?'

'Perhaps,' said the other slowly, as he explored the safe with an electric torch, 'perhaps they didn't require much of that. My word! it strikes warm coming out of that place! like a vault, it is. But here, what's this bank-like of dust all spread out into the room? That must have come there since the door was opened; it would sweep it all away if you moved it—see? Now what do you make of that?'

'Make of it? About as much as I make of anything else in this case. One of London's mysteries this is going to be, by what I can see, and I don't believe a photographer's box full of large-size old fashioned Prayer-Books is going to take us much further. For that's just what your package is.'

It was a natural but hasty utterance. The preceding narrative shows that there was in fact plenty of material for constructing a case; and when once Messrs. Davidson and Witham had brought their end to Scotland Yard, the join-up was soon made, and the circle completed.

To the relief of Mrs Porter, the owners of Brockstone decided not to replace the books in the chapel: they repose, I believe, in a safe-deposit in town. The police have their own methods of keeping certain matters out of the newspapers: otherwise it can hardly be supposed that Watkins's evidence about Mr Poschwitz's death could have failed to furnish a good many headlines of a startling character to the press.

# A Neighbour's Landmark

Those who spend the greater part of their time in reading or writing books are, of course, apt to take rather particular notice of accumulations of books when they come across them. They will not pass a stall, a shop, or even a bedroom-shelf without reading some title, and if they find themselves in an unfamiliar library, no host need trouble himself further about their entertainment. The putting of dispersed sets of volumes together, or the turning right way up of those which the dusting housemaid has left in an apoplectic condition, appeals to them as one of the lesser Works of Mercy. Happy in these employments, and in occasionally opening an eighteenth-century octavo, to see 'what it is all about', and to conclude after five minutes that it deserves the seclusion it now enjoys, I had reached the middle of a wet August afternoon at Betton Court—

'You begin in a deeply Victorian manner,' I said; 'is this to continue?'

'Remember, if you please,' said my friend, looking at me over his spectacles, 'that I am a Victorian by birth and education, and that the Victorian tree may not unreasonably be expected to bear Victorian fruit. Further, remember that an immense quantity of clever and thoughtful rubbish is now being written about the Victorian age. Now,' he went on, laying his papers on his knee, 'that article, "The Stricken Years", in The

43

Times Literary Supplement the other day,—able? of course it is able; but, oh! my soul and body, do just hand it over here, will you? it's on the table by you.'

'I thought you were to read me something you had written,' I said, without moving, 'but, of course—'

'Yes, I know,' he said. 'Very well, then, I'll do that first. But I should like to show you afterwards what I mean. However—' And he lifted the sheets of paper and adjusted his spectacles.

—at Betton Court, where, generations back, two country-house libraries had been fused together, and no descendant of either stock had ever faced the task of picking them over or getting rid of duplicates. Now I am not setting out to tell of rarities I may have discovered, of Shakespeare quartos bound up in volumes of political tracts, or anything of that kind, but of an experience which befell me in the course of my search—an experience which I cannot either explain away or fit into the scheme of my ordinary life.

It was, I said, a wet August afternoon, rather windy, rather warm. Outside the window great trees were stirring and weeping. Between them were stretches of green and yellow country (for the Court stands high on a hill-side), and blue hills far off, veiled with rain. Up above was a very restless and hopeless movement of low clouds travelling northwest. I had suspended my work—if you call it work—for some minutes to stand at the window and look at these things, and at the greenhouse roof on the right with the water sliding off it, and the Church tower that rose behind that. It was all in favour of my going steadily on; no likelihood of a clearing up for hours to come. I, therefore, returned to the shelves, lifted out a set of eight or nine volumes, lettered Tracts, and conveyed them to the table for closer examination.

They were for the most part of the reign of Anne. There was a good deal of The Late Peace, The Late War, The Conduct of the Allies: there were also Letters to a Convocation Man; Sermons preached at St Michael's, Queen hithe; Enquiries in to a late Charge of the Rt. Rev. the Lord Bishop of Winchester (or more probably Winton) to his Clergy: things all very lively once, and indeed still keeping so much of their old sting that I was tempted to betake myself into an arm-chair in the window, and give them more time than I had intended. Besides, I was somewhat tired by the day. The Church clock struck four, and it really was four, for in 1889 there was no saving of daylight.

So I settled myself. And first I glanced over some of the War pamphlets, and pleased myself by trying to pick out Swift by his style from among the undistinguished. But the War pamphlets needed more knowledge of the geography of the Low Countries than I had. I turned to the Church, and read several pages of what the Dean of Canterbury said to the Society for Promoting Christian Knowledge on the occasion of their anniversary meeting in 1711. When I turned over to a Letter from a Beneficed Clergyman in the Country to the Bishop of C— —r, I was becoming languid, and I gazed for some moments at the following sentence without surprise:

'This Abuse (for I think myself justified in calling it by that name) is one which I am persuaded Your Lordship would (if 'twere known to you) exert your utmost efforts to do away. But I am also persuaded that you know no more of its existence than (in the words of the Country Song)

That which walks in Betton Wood Knows why it walks or why it cries.'

Then indeed I did sit up in my chair, and run my finger along the lines to make sure that I had read them right. There was no mistake. Nothing more was to be gathered from the rest of the pamphlet. The next paragraph definitely changed the subject: 'But I have said enough upon this Topick' were its opening words. So discreet, too, was the namelessness of the Beneficed Clergyman that he refrained even from initials, and had his letter printed in London.

The riddle was of a kind that might faintly interest anyone: to me, who have dabbled a good deal in works of folk-lore, it was really exciting. I was set upon solving it—on finding out, I mean, what story lay behind it; and, at least, I felt myself lucky in one point, that, whereas I might have come on the paragraph in some College Library far away, here I was at Betton, on the very scene of action.

The Church clock struck five, and a single stroke on a gong followed. This, I knew, meant tea. I heaved myself out of the deep chair, and obeyed the summons.

My host and I were alone at the Court. He came in soon, wet from a round of landlord's errands, and with pieces of local news which had to be passed on before I could make an opportunity of asking whether there was a particular place in the parish that was still known as Betton Wood.
'Betton Wood,' he said, 'was a short mile away, just on the crest of Betton Hill, and my father stubbed up the last bit of it when it paid better to grow corn than scrub oaks. Why do you want to know about Betton Wood?'

'Because,' I said, 'in an old pamphlet I was reading just now, there are two lines of a country song which mention it, and they sound as if there was a story belonging to them.

Someone says that someone else knows no more of whatever
it may be—

Than that which walks in Betton Wood Knows why it walks
or why it cries.'

'Goodness,' said Philipson, 'I wonder whether that was
why...I must ask old Mitchell.' He muttered something else to
himself, and took some more tea, thoughtfully.

'Whether that was why—?' I said.

'Yes, I was going to say, whether that was why my father had
the Wood stubbed up. I said just now it was to get more
plough-land, but I don't really know if it was. I don't believe
he ever broke it up: it's rough pasture at this moment. But
there's one old chap at least who'd remember something of
it—old Mitchell.' He looked at his watch. 'Blest if I don't go
down there and ask him. I don't think I'll take you,' he went
on; 'he's not so likely to tell anything he thinks is odd if there's
a stranger by.'

'Well, mind you remember every single thing he does tell. As
for me, if it clears up, I shall go out, and if it doesn't, I shall go
on with the books.'
It did clear up, sufficiently at least to make me think it worth
while to walk up the nearest hill and look over the country. I
did not know the lie of the land; it was the first visit I had
paid to Philipson, and this was the first day of it. So I went
down the garden and through the wet shrubberies with a
very open mind, and offered no resistance to the indistinct
impulse—was it, however, so very indistinct?—which kept
urging me to bear to the left whenever there was a forking of
the path. The result was that after ten minutes or more of

dark going between dripping rows of box and laurel and privet, I was confronted by a stone arch in the Gothic style set in the stone wall which encircled the whole demesne. The door was fastened by a spring-lock, and I took the precaution of leaving this on the jar as I passed out into the road. That road I crossed, and entered a narrow lane between hedges which led upward; and that lane I pursued at a leisurely pace for as much as half a mile, and went on to the field to which it led. I was now on a good point of vantage for taking in the situation of the Court, the village, and the environment; and I leant upon a gate and gazed westward and downward.

I think we must all know the landscapes—are they by Birket Foster, or somewhat earlier?—which, in the form of wood-cuts, decorate the volumes of poetry that lay on the drawing-room tables of our fathers and grandfathers—volumes in 'Art Cloth, embossed bindings'; that strikes me as being the right phrase. I confess myself an admirer of them, and especially of those which show the peasant leaning over a gate in a hedge and surveying, at the bottom of a downward slope, the village church spire—embosomed amid venerable trees, and a fertile plain intersected by hedgerows, and bounded by distant hills, behind which the orb of day is sinking (or it may be rising) amid level clouds illumined by his dying (or nascent) ray. The expressions employed here are those which seem appropriate to the pictures I have in mind; and were there opportunity, I would try to work in the Vale, the Grove, the Cot, and the Flood. Anyhow, they are beautiful to me, these landscapes, and it was just such a one that I was now surveying. It might have come straight out of Gems of Sacred Song, selected by a Lady and given as a birthday present to Eleanor Philipson in 1852 by her attached friend Millicent Graves. All at once I turned as if I had been stung. There thrilled into my right ear and pierced my head a note of incredible sharpness, like the shriek of a bat, only ten times intensified—the kind of thing that makes one wonder if something has not given way in one's brain. I held my breath, and covered my ear, and shivered. Something in the circulation: another minute or two, I thought, and I return home. But I must fix the view a little more firmly in my mind. Only, when I turned to it again, the taste was gone out of it. The sun was down behind the hill, and the light was off the fields, and when the clock bell in the Church tower struck seven, I thought no longer of kind mellow evening hours of rest, and scents of flowers and woods on evening air; and of how someone on a farm a mile or two off would be saying 'How clear Betton bell sounds tonight after the rain!'; but instead images came to me of dusty beams and creeping spiders and savage owls up in the tower, and forgotten graves and their ugly contents below, and of flying Time and all it had taken out of my life. And just then into my left ear—close as if lips had been put within an inch of my head, the frightful scream came thrilling again.

There was no mistake possible now. It was from outside. 'With no language but a cry' was the thought that flashed into my mind. Hideous it was beyond anything I had heard or have heard since, but I could read no emotion in it, and doubted if I could read any intelligence. All its effect was to take away every vestige, every possibility, of enjoyment, and make this no place to stay in one moment more. Of course there was nothing to be seen: but I was convinced that, if I waited, the thing would pass me again on its aimless, endless beat, and I could not bear the notion of a third repetition. I hurried back to the lane and down the hill. But when I came to the arch in the wall I stopped. Could I be sure of my way among those dank alleys, which would be danker and darker now! No, I confessed to myself that I was afraid: so jarred were all my nerves with the cry on the hill that I really felt I could not afford to be startled even by a little bird in a bush, or a rabbit. I followed the road which followed the wall, and I was not sorry when I came to the gate and the lodge, and descried Philipson coming up towards it from the direction of the village.

'And where have you been?' said he.

'I took that lane that goes up the hill opposite the stone arch in the wall.'

'Oh! did you? Then you've been very near where Betton Wood used to be: at least, if you followed it up to the top, and out into the field.'

And if the reader will believe it, that was the first time that I put two and two together. Did I at once tell Philipson what had happened to me? I did not. I have not had other experiences of the kind which are called super-natural, or -normal, or -physical, but, though I knew very well I must speak of this one before long, I was not at all anxious to do so; and I think I have read that this is a common case.

So all I said was: 'Did you see the old man you meant to?'

'Old Mitchell? Yes, I did; and got something of a story out of him. I'll keep it till after dinner. It really is rather odd.'

So when we were settled after dinner he began to report, faithfully, as he said, the dialogue that had taken place. Mitchell, not far off eighty years old, was in his elbow-chair. The married daughter with whom he lived was in and out preparing for tea.

50

After the usual salutations: 'Mitchell, I want you to tell me something about the Wood.'

'What Wood's that, Master Reginald?'

'Betton Wood. Do you remember it?'

Mitchell slowly raised his hand and pointed an accusing forefinger. 'It were your father done away with Betton Wood, Master Reginald, I can tell you that much.'

'Well, I know it was, Mitchell. You needn't look at me as if it were my fault.'

'Your fault? No, I says it were your father done it, before your time.'

'Yes, and I dare say if the truth was known, it was your father that advised him to do it, and I want to know why.' Mitchell seemed a little amused. 'Well,' he said, 'my father were woodman to your father and your grandfather before him, and if he didn't know what belonged to his business, he'd oughter done. And if he did give advice that way, I suppose he might have had his reasons, mightn't he now?'

'Of course he might, and I want you to tell me what they were.'

'Well now, Master Reginald, whatever makes you think as I know what his reasons might 'a been I don't know how many year ago?'

'Well, to be sure, it is a long time, and you might easily have

51

forgotten, if ever you knew. I suppose the only thing is for me to go and ask old Ellis what he can recollect about it.'

That had the effect I hoped for.

'Old Ellis!' he growled. 'First time ever I hear anyone say old Ellis were any use for any purpose. I should 'a thought you know'd better than that yourself, Master Reginald. What do you suppose old Ellis can tell you better'n what I can about Betton Wood, and what call have he got to be put afore me, I should like to know. His father warn't woodman on the place: he were ploughman—that's what he was, and so anyone could tell you what knows; anyone could tell you that, I says.'

'Just so, Mitchell, but if you know all about Betton Wood and won't tell me, why, I must do the next best I can, and try and get it out of somebody else; and old Ellis has been on the place very nearly as long as you have.'

'That he ain't, not by eighteen months! Who says I wouldn't tell you nothing about the Wood? I ain't no objection; only it's a funny kind of a tale, and 'taint right to my thinkin' it should be all about the parish. You, Lizzie, do you keep in your kitchen a bit. Me and Master Reginald wants to have a word or two private. But one thing I'd like to know, Master Reginald, what come to put you upon asking about it today?'

'Oh! well, I happened to hear of an old saying about something that walks in Betton Wood. And I wondered if that had anything to do with its being cleared away: that's all.'

'Well, you was in the right, Master Reginald, however you come to hear of it, and I believe I can tell you the rights of it better than anyone in this parish, let alone old Ellis. You see it

52

came about this way: that the shortest road to Allen's Farm laid through the Wood, and when we was little my poor mother she used to go so many times in the week to the farm to fetch a quart of milk, because Mr Allen what had the farm then under your father, he was a good man, and anyone that had a young family to bring up, he was willing to allow 'em so much in the week. But never you mind about that now. And my poor mother she never liked to go through the Wood, because there was a lot of talk in the place, and sayings like what you spoke about just now. But every now and again, when she happened to be late with her work, she'd have to take the short road through the Wood, and as sure as ever she did, she'd come home in a rare state. I remember her and my father talking about it, and he'd say, "Well, but it can't do you no harm, Emma," and she'd say, "Oh! but you haven't an idear of it, George. Why, it went right through my head," she says, "and I came over all bewildered-like, and as if I didn't know where I was. You see, George," she says, "it ain't as if you was about there in the dusk. You always goes there in the daytime, now don't you?" and he says: "Why, to be sure I do; do you take me for a fool?" And so they'd go on. And time passed by, and I think it wore her out, because, you understand, it warn't no use to go for the milk not till the afternoon, and she wouldn't never send none of us children instead, for fear we should get a fright. Nor she wouldn't tell us about it herself. "No," she says, "it's bad enough for me. I don't want no one else to go through it, nor yet hear talk about it." But one time I recollect she says, "Well, first it's a rustling-like all along in the bushes, coming very quick, either towards me or after me according to the time, and then there comes this scream as appears to pierce right through from the one ear to the other, and the later I am coming through, the more like I am to hear it twice over; but thanks be, I never yet heard it the three times." And then I asked her, and I says: "Why, that seems like someone walking to and fro all the time, don't it?" and she says, "Yes, it do, and whatever it is she wants, I can't think": and I says, "Is it a woman, mother?" and she says, "Yes, I've heard it is a woman."

'Anyway, the end of it was my father he spoke to your father, and told him the Wood was a bad wood. "There's never a bit of game in it, and there's never a bird's nest there," he says, "and it ain't no manner of use to you." And after a lot of talk, your father he come and see my mother about it, and he see she warn't one of these silly women as gets nervish about nothink at all, and he made up his mind there was somethink in it, and after that he asked about in the neighbourhood, and I believe he made out somethink, and wrote it down in a paper what very like you've got up at the Court, Master Reginald. And then he gave the order, and the Wood was stubbed up. They done all the work in the daytime, I recollect, and was never there after three o'clock.' 'Didn't they find anything to explain it, Mitchell? No bones or anything of that kind?'

'Nothink at all, Master Reginald, only the mark of a hedge and ditch along the middle, much about where the quickset hedge run now; and with all the work they done, if there had been anyone put away there, they was bound to find 'em. But I don't know whether it done much good, after all. People here don't seem to like the place no better than they did afore.'

'That's about what I got out of Mitchell,' said Philipson, 'and as far as any explanation goes, it leaves us very much where we were. I must see if I can't find that paper.'

'Why didn't your father ever tell you about the business?' I said.

54

'He died before I went to school, you know, and I imagine he didn't want to frighten us children by any such story. I can remember being shaken and slapped by my nurse for running up that lane towards the Wood when we were coming back rather late one winter afternoon: but in the daytime no one interfered with our going into the Wood if we wanted to— only we never did want.'

'Hm!' I said, and then, 'Do you you think you'll be able to find that paper that your father wrote?'

'Yes,' he said, 'I do. I expect it's no farther away than that cupboard behind you. There's a bundle or two of things specially put aside, most of which I've looked through at various times, and I know there's one envelope labelled Betton Wood: but as there was no Betton Wood any more, I never thought it would be worth while to open it, and I never have. We'll do it now, though.'

'Before you do,' I said (I was still reluctant, but I thought this was perhaps the moment for my disclosure), 'I'd better tell you I think Mitchell was right when he doubted if clearing away the Wood had put things straight.' And I gave the account you have heard already: I need not say Philipson was interested. 'Still there?' he said. 'It's amazing. Look here, will you come out there with me now, and see what happens?'

'I will do no such thing,' I said, 'and if you knew the feeling, you'd be glad to walk ten miles in the opposite direction. Don't talk of it. Open your envelope, and let's hear what your father made out.'

He did so, and read me the three or four pages of jottings

which it contained. At the top was written a motto from Scott's Glenfinlas, which seemed to me well-chosen:

Where walks, they say, the shrieking ghost.

Then there were notes of his talk with Mitchell's mother, from which I extract only this much. 'I asked her if she never thought she saw anything to account for the sounds she heard. She told me, no more than once, on the darkest evening she ever came through the Wood; and then she seemed forced to look behind her as the rustling came in the bushes, and she thought she saw something all in tatters with the two arms held out in front of it coming on very fast, and at that she ran for the stile, and tore her gown all to finders getting over it.'

Then he had gone to two other people whom he found very shy of talking. They seemed to think, among other things, that it reflected discredit on the parish. However, one, Mrs Emma Frost, was prevailed upon to repeat what her mother had told her. 'They say it was a lady of title that married twice over, and her first husband went by the name of Brown, or it might have been Bryan ['Yes, there were Bryans at the Court before it came into our family,' Philipson put in], and she removed her neighbour's landmark: leastways she took in a fair piece of the best pasture in Betton parish what belonged by rights to two children as hadn't no one to speak for them, and they say years after she went from bad to worse, and made out false papers to gain thousands of pounds up in London, and at last they was proved in law to be false, and she would have been tried and put to death very like, only she escaped away for the time. But no one can't avoid the curse that's laid on them that removes the landmark, and so we take it she can't leave Betton before someone take and put it right again.'

56

At the end of the paper there was a note to this effect. 'I regret that I cannot find any clue to previous owners of the fields adjoining the Wood. I do not hesitate to say that if I could discover their representatives, I should do my best to indemnify them for the wrong done to them in years now long past: for it is undeniable that the Wood is very curiously disturbed in the manner described by the people of the place. In my present ignorance alike of the extent of the land wrongly appropriated, and of the rightful owners, I am reduced to keeping a separate note of the profits derived from this part of the estate, and my custom has been to apply the sum that would represent the annual yield of about five acres to the common benefit of the parish and to charitable uses: and I hope that those who succeed me may see fit to continue this practice.'

So much for the elder Mr Philipson's paper. To those who, like myself, are readers of the State Trials it will have gone far to illuminate the situation. They will remember how between the years 1678 and 1684 the Lady Ivy, formerly Theodosia Bryan, was alternately Plaintiff and Defendant in a series of trials in which she was trying to establish a claim against the Dean and Chapter of St Paul's for a considerable and very valuable tract of land in Shadwell: how in the last of those trials, presided over by L. C. J. Jeffreys, it was proved up to the hilt that the deeds upon which she based her claim were forgeries executed under her orders: and how, after an information for perjury and forgery was issued against her, she disappeared completely—so completely, indeed, that no expert has ever been able to tell me what became of her.

Does not the story I have told suggest that she may still be heard of on the scene of one of her earlier and more successful exploits?

\* \* \*

'That,' said my friend, as he folded up his papers, 'is a very faithful record of my one extraordinary experience. And now—'

But I had so many questions to ask him, as for instance, whether his friend had found the proper owner of the land, whether he had done anything about the hedge, whether the sounds were ever heard now, what was the exact title and date of his pamphlet, etc., etc., that bed-time came and passed, without his having an opportunity to revert to the Literary Supplement of The Times.

[Thanks to the researches of Sir John Fox, in his book on The Lady Ivie's Trial (Oxford, 1929), we now know that my heroine died in her bed in 1695, having—heaven knows how—been acquitted of the forgery, for which she had undoubtedly been responsible.]

# RATS

'And if you was to walk through the bedrooms now, you'd see the ragged, mouldy bedclothes a-heaving and a-heaving like seas.' 'And a-heaving and a-heaving with what?' he says. 'Why, with the rats under 'em.'

But was it with the rats? I ask, because in another case it was not. I cannot put a date to the story, but I was young when I heard it, and the teller was old. It is an ill-proportioned tale, but that is my fault, not his.

It happened in Suffolk, near the coast. In a place where the road makes a sudden dip and then a sudden rise; as you go northward, at the top of that rise, stands a house on the left of the road. It is a tall red-brick house, narrow for its height; perhaps it was built about 1770. The top of the front has a low triangular pediment with a round window in the centre. Behind it are stables and offices, and such garden as it has is behind them. Scraggy Scotch firs are near it: an expanse of gorse-covered land stretches away from it. It commands a view of the distant sea from the upper windows of the front. A sign on a post stands before the door; or did so stand, for though it was an inn of repute once, I believe it is so no longer.

To this inn came my acquaintance, Mr Thomson, when he was a young man, on a fine spring day, coming from the University of Cambridge, and desirous of solitude in tolerable quarters and time for reading. These he found, for the landlord and his wife had been in service and could make a visitor comfortable, and there was no one else staying in the inn. He had a large room on the first floor commanding the road and the view, and if it faced east, why, that could not be helped; the house was well built and warm.

He spent very tranquil and uneventful days: work all the morning, an afternoon perambulation of the country round, a little conversation with country company or the people of the inn in the evening over the then fashionable drink of brandy and water, a little more reading and writing, and bed; and he would have been content that this should continue for the full month he had at disposal, so well was his work progressing, and so fine was the April of that year—which I have reason to believe was that which Orlando Whistlecraft chronicles in his weather record as the 'Charming Year'.

One of his walks took him along the northern road, which stands high and traverses a wide common, called a heath. On the bright afternoon when he first chose this direction his eye caught a white object some hundreds of yards to the left of the road, and he felt it necessary to make sure what this might be. It was not long before he was standing by it, and found himself looking at a square block of white stone fashioned somewhat like the base of a pillar, with a square hole in the upper surface. Just such another you may see at this day on Thetford Heath. After taking stock of it he contemplated for a few minutes the view, which offered a church tower or two, some red roofs of cottages and windows winking in the sun, and the expanse of sea—also with an occasional wink and gleam upon it—and so pursued his way.

In the desultory evening talk in the bar, he asked why the white stone was there on the common.

'A old-fashioned thing, that is,' said the landlord (Mr Betts), 'we was none of us alive when that was put there.' 'That's right,' said another. 'It stands pretty high,' said Mr Thomson, 'I dare say a sea-mark was on it some time back.' 'Ah! yes,' Mr Betts agreed, 'I 'ave 'eard they could see it from the boats; but whatever there was, it's fell to bits this long time.' 'Good job too,' said a third, "twarn't a lucky mark, by what the old men used to say; not lucky for the fishin', I mean to say.' 'Why ever not?' said Thomson. 'Well, I never see it myself,' was the answer, 'but they 'ad some funny ideas, what I mean, peculiar, them old chaps, and I shouldn't wonder but what they made away with it theirselves.'

It was impossible to get anything clearer than this: the company, never very voluble, fell silent, and when next someone spoke it was of village affairs and crops. Mr Betts was the speaker.

Not every day did Thomson consult his health by taking a country walk. One very fine afternoon found him busily writing at three o'clock. Then he stretched himself and rose, and walked out of his room into the passage. Facing him was another room, then the stair-head, then two more rooms, one looking out to the back, the other to the south. At the south end of the passage was a window, to which he went, considering with himself that it was rather a shame to waste such a fine afternoon. However, work was paramount just at the moment; he thought he would just take five minutes off and go back to it, and those five minutes he would employ—the Bettses could not possibly object—to looking at the other rooms in the passage, which he had never seen. Nobody at all, it seemed, was indoors; probably, as it was market day, they were all gone to the town, except perhaps a maid in the bar. Very still the house was, and the sun shone really hot;

early flies buzzed in the window-panes. So he explored. The room facing his own was undistinguished except for an old print of Bury St Edmunds; the two next him on his side of the passage were gay and clean, with one window apiece, whereas his had two. Remained the south-west room, opposite to the last which he had entered. This was locked; but Thomson was in a mood of quite indefensible curiosity, and feeling confident that there could be no damaging secrets in a place so easily got at, he proceeded to fetch the key of his own room, and when that did not answer, to collect the keys of the other three. One of them fitted, and he opened the door. The room had two windows looking south and west, so it was as bright and the sun as hot upon it as could be. Here there was no carpet, but bare boards; no pictures, no washing-stand, only a bed, in the farther corner: an iron bed, with mattress and bolster, covered with a bluish check counterpane. As featureless a room as you can well imagine, and yet there was something that made Thomson close the door very quickly and yet quietly behind him and lean against the window-sill in the passage, actually quivering all over. It was this, that under the counterpane someone lay, and not only lay, but stirred. That it was some one and not some thing was certain, because the shape of a head was unmistakable on the bolster; and yet it was all covered, and no one lies with covered head but a dead person; and this was not dead, not truly dead, for it heaved and shivered. If he had seen these things in dusk or by the light of a flickering candle, Thomson could have comforted himself and talked of fancy. On this bright day that was impossible. What was to be done? First, lock the door at all costs. Very gingerly he approached it and bending down listened, holding his breath; perhaps there might be a sound of heavy breathing, and a prosaic explanation. There was absolute silence. But as, with a rather tremulous hand, he put the key into its hole and turned it, it rattled, and on the instant a stumbling padding tread was heard coming towards the door. Thomson fled like a rabbit to his room and locked himself in: futile enough, he knew it was; would doors and locks be any obstacle to what he suspected? but it was all he could think of at the moment, and in fact nothing happened; only there was a time of acute suspense—followed by a misery of doubt as to what to do. The impulse, of course, was to slip away as soon as possible from a house which contained such an inmate. But only the day before he had said he should be staying for at least a week more, and how if he changed plans could he avoid the suspicion of having pried into places where he certainly had no business? Moreover, either the Bettses knew all about the inmate, and yet did not leave the house, or knew nothing, which equally meant that there was nothing to be afraid of, or knew just enough to make them shut up the room, but not enough to weigh on their spirits: in any of these cases it seemed that not much was to be feared, and certainly so far as he had had no sort of ugly experience. On the whole the line of least resistance was to stay.

Well, he stayed out his week. Nothing took him past that door, and, often as he would pause in a quiet hour of day or night in the passage and listen, and listen, no sound whatever issued from that direction. You might have thought that Thomson would have made some attempt at ferreting out stories connected with the inn—hardly perhaps from Betts, but from the parson of the parish, or old people in the village; but no, the reticence which commonly falls on people who have had strange experiences, and believe in them, was upon him. Nevertheless, as the end of his stay drew near, his yearning after some kind of explanation grew more and more acute. On his solitary walks he persisted in planning out some way, the least obtrusive, of getting another daylight glimpse into that room, and eventually arrived at this scheme. He would leave by an afternoon train—about four o'clock. When his fly was waiting, and his luggage on it, he would make one last expedition upstairs to look round his own room and see if anything was left unpacked, and then, with that key, which he had contrived to oil (as if that made any difference!), the door should once more be opened, for a moment, and shut.

So it worked out. The bill was paid, the consequent small talk gone through while the fly was loaded: 'pleasant part of the country—been very comfortable, thanks to you and Mrs Betts—hope to come back some time', on one side: on the other, 'very glad you've found satisfaction, sir, done our best—always glad to 'ave your good word—very much favoured we've been with the weather, to be sure.' Then, 'I'll just take a look upstairs in case I've left a book or something out—no, don't trouble, I'll be back in a minute.' And as noiselessly as possible he stole to the door and opened it. The shattering of the illusion! He almost laughed aloud. Propped, or you might say sitting, on the edge of the bed was—nothing in the round world but a scarecrow! A scarecrow out of the garden, of course, dumped into the deserted room...Yes; but here amusement ceased. Have scarecrows bare bony feet? Do their heads loll on to their shoulders? Have they iron collars and links of chain about their necks? Can they get up and move, if never so stiffly, across a floor, with wagging head and arms close at their sides? and shiver?

The slam of the door, the dash to the stair-head, the leap downstairs, were followed by a faint. Awakening, Thomson saw Betts standing over him with the brandy bottle and a very reproachful face. 'You shouldn't a done so, sir, really you shouldn't. It ain't a kind way to act by persons as done the best they could for you.' Thomson heard words of this kind, but what he said in reply he did not know. Mr Betts, and perhaps even more Mrs Betts, found it hard to accept his apologies and his assurances that he would say no word that could damage the good name of the house. However, they were accepted. Since the train could not now be caught, it was arranged that Thomson should be driven to the town to sleep there. Before he went the Bettses told him what little they knew. 'They says he was landlord 'ere a long time back, and was in with the 'ighwaymen that 'ad their beat about the 'eath. That's how he come by his end: 'ung in chains, they say, up where you see that stone what the gallus stood in. Yes, the fishermen made away with that, I believe, because they see it out at sea and it kep' the fish off, according to their idea. Yes, we 'ad the account from the people that 'ad the 'ouse before we come. "You keep that room shut up," they says, "but don't move the bed out, and you'll find there won't be no trouble." And no more there 'as been; not once he haven't come out into the 'ouse, though what he may do now there ain't no sayin'. Anyway, you're the first I know on that's seen him since we've been 'ere: I never set eyes on him myself, nor don't want. And ever since we've made the servants' rooms in the stablin', we ain't 'ad no difficulty that way. Only I do 'ope, sir, as you'll keep a close tongue, considerin' 'ow an 'ouse do get talked about': with more to this effect.

The promise of silence was kept for many years. The occasion of my hearing the story at last was this: that when Mr Thomson came to stay with my father it fell to me to show him to his room, and instead of letting me open the door for him, he stepped forward and threw it open himself, and then for some moments stood in the doorway holding up his candle and looking narrowly into the interior. Then he seemed to recollect himself and said: 'I beg your pardon. Very absurd, but I can't help doing that, for a particular reason.'

What that reason was I heard some days afterwards, and you have heard now.

# THE EXPERIMENT

## A NEW YEAR'S EVE GHOST STORY

The Reverend Dr Hall was in his study making up the entries for the year in the parish register: it being his custom to note baptisms, weddings and burials in a paper book as they occurred, and in the last days of December to write them out fairly in the vellum book that was kept in the parish chest.

To him entered his housekeeper, in evident agitation. 'Oh, sir,' said she, 'whatever do you think? The poor Squire's gone!'

'The Squire? Squire Bowles? What are you talking about, woman? Why, only yesterday—.'

'Yes, I know, sir, but it's the truth. Wickem, the clerk, just left word on his way down to toll the bell—you'll hear it yourself in a minute. There now, just listen.'

Sure enough the sound broke on the still night—not loud, for the Rectory did not immediately adjoin the churchyard. Dr Hall rose hastily.

'Terrible, terrible,' he said. 'I must see them at the Hall at once. He seemed so greatly better yesterday.' He paused. 'Did you hear any word of the sickness having come this way at all? There was nothing said in Norwich. It seems so sudden.'

'No, indeed, sir, no such thing. Just caught away with a choking in his throat, Wickem says. It do make one feel—

67

well, I'm sure I had to set down as much as a minute or more, I come over that queer when I heard the words—and by what I could understand they'll be asking for the burial very quick. There's some can't bear the thought of the cold corpse laying in the house, and—.'

'Yes: well, I must find out from Madam Bowles herself or Mr Joseph. Get me my cloak, will you? Ah, and could you let Wickem know that I desire to see him when the tolling is over?' He hurried off.

'In an hour's time he was back and found Wickem waiting for him. 'There is work for you, Wickem,' he said, as he threw off his cloak, 'and not overmuch time to do it in.'

'Yes, sir,' said Wickem, 'the vault to be opened to be sure—.'

'No, no, that's not the message I have. The poor Squire, they tell me, charged them before now not to lay him in the chancel. It was to be an earth grave in the yard, on the north side.' He stopped at an inarticulate exclamation from the clerk. 'Well?' he said.

'I ask pardon, sir,' said Wickem in a shocked voice, 'but did I understand you right? No vault, you say, and on the north side? Tt-tt-! Why the poor gentleman must a been wandering.' 'Yes, it does seem strange to me, too,' said Dr Hall, 'but no, Mr Joseph tells me it was his father's—I should say stepfather's—clear wish, expressed more than once, and when he was in good health. Clean earth and open air. You know, of course, the poor Squire had his fancies, though he never spoke of this one to me. And there's another thing, Wickem. No coffin.'

'Oh dear, dear, sir,' said Wickem, yet more shocked. 'Oh, but that'll make sad talk, that will, and what a disappointment for Wright, too! I know he'd looked out some beautiful wood for the Squire, and had it by him years past.'

'Well, well, perhaps the family will make it up to Wright in some way,' said the Rector, rather impatiently, 'but what you have to do is to get the grave dug and all things in a readiness—torches from Wright you must not forget—by ten o'clock tomorrow night. I don't doubt but there will be somewhat coming to you for your pains and hurry.'

'Very well, sir, if those be the orders, I must do my best to carry them out. And should I call in on my way down and send the women up to the Hall to lay out the body, sir?'

'No: that, I think—I am sure—was not spoken of. Mr Joseph will send, no doubt, if they are needed. No, you have enough without that. Good-night, Wickem. I was making up the registers when this doleful news came. Little had I thought to add such an entry to them as I must now.'

 All things had been done in decent order. The torchlighted cortege had passed from the Hall through the park, up the lime avenue to the top of the knoll on which the church stood. All the village had been there, and such neighbours as could be warned in the few hours available. There was no great surprise at the hurry.

Formalities of law there were none then, and no one blamed the stricken widow for hastening to lay her dead to rest. Nor did anyone look to see her following in the funeral train. Her son Joseph—only issue of her first marriage with a Calvert of Yorkshire—was the chief mourner.

There were, indeed, no kinsfolk on Squire Bowles's side who could have been bidden. The will, executed at the time of the Squire's second marriage, left everything to the widow.

And what was 'everything'? Land, house, furniture, pictures, plate were all obvious. But there should have been accumulations in coin, and beyond a few hundreds in the hands of agents—honest men and no embezzlers—cash there was none. Yet Francis Bowles had for years received good rents and paid little out. Nor was he a reputed miser; he kept a good table, and money was always forthcoming for the moderate spendings of his wife and stepson. Joseph Calvert had been maintained ungrudgingly at school and college.

What, then, had he done with it all? No ransacking of the house brought any secret hoard to light; no servant, old or young, had any tale to tell of meeting the Squire in unexpected places at strange hours. No, Madam Bowles and her son were fairly non-plussed. As they sat one evening in the parlour discussing the problem for the twentieth time: 'You have been at his books and papers, Joseph, again today, haven't you?'

'Yes, mother, and no forwarder.'

'What was it he would be writing at, and why was he always sending letters to Mr Fowler at Gloucester?'

'Why, you know he had a maggot about the Middle State of the Soul. 'Twas over that he and that other were always busy. The last thing he wrote would be a letter that he never finished. I'll fetch it...Yes, the same song over again.

"'Honoured friend,—I make some slow advance in our

70

studies, but I know not well how far to trust our authors. Here is one lately come my way who will have it that for a time after death the soul is under control of certain spirits, as Raphael, and another whom I doubtfully read as Nares; but still so near to this state of life that on prayer to them he may be free to come and disclose matters to the living. Come, indeed, he must, if he be rightly called, the manner of which is set forth in an experiment. But having come, and once opened his mouth, it may chance that his summoner shall see and hear more than of the hid treasure which it is likely he bargained for; since the experiment puts this in the forefront of things to be enquired. But the eftest way is to send you the whole, which herewith I do; copied from a book of recipes which I had of good Bishop Moore.'''

Here Joseph stopped, and made no comment, gazing on the paper. For more than a minute nothing was said, then Madam Bowles, drawing her needle through her work and looking at it, coughed and said, 'There was no more written?'

'No, nothing, mother.'

'No? Well, it is strange stuff. Did ever you meet this Mr Fowler?'

'Yes, it might be once or twice, in Oxford, a civil gentleman enough.'

'Now I think of it,' said she, 'it would be but right to acquaint him with—with what has happened: they were close friends. Yes, Joseph, you should do that: you will know what should be said. And the letter is his, after all.'

'You are in the right, mother, and I'll not delay it.' And forthwith he sat down to write.

From Norfolk to Gloucester was no quick transit. But a letter went, and a larger packet came in answer; and there were more evening talks in the panelled parlour at the Hall. At the close of one, these words were said: 'Tonight, then, if you are certain of yourself, go round by the field path. Ay, and here is a cloth will serve.'

'What cloth is that, mother? A napkin?'

'Yes, of a kind: what matter?' So he went out by the way of the garden, and she stood in the door, musing, with her hand on her mouth. Then the hand dropped and she said half aloud: 'If only I had not been so hurried! But it was the face cloth, sure enough.'
It was a very dark night, and the spring wind blew loud over the black fields: loud enough to drown all sounds of shouting or calling. If calling there was, there was no voice, nor any that answered, nor any that regarded—yet.

Next morning, Joseph's mother was early in his chamber. 'Give me the cloth,' she said, 'the maids must not find it. And tell me, tell me, quick!'

Joseph, seated on the side of the bed with his head in his hands, looked up at her with bloodshot eyes. 'We have opened his mouth,' he said. 'Why in God's name did you leave his face bare?'

'How could I help it? You know how I was hurried that day? But do you mean you saw it?'

Joseph only groaned and sunk his head in his hands again. Then, in a low voice, 'He said you should see it, too.'

72

With a dreadful gasp she clutched at the bedpost and clung to it. 'Oh, but he's angry,' Joseph went on. 'He was only biding his time, I'm sure. The words were scarce out of my mouth when I heard like the snarl of a dog in under there.' He got up and paced the room. 'And what can we do? He's free! And I daren't meet him! I daren't take the drink and go where he is! I daren't lie here another night. Oh, why did you do it? We could have waited.'

'Hush,' said his mother: her lips were dry. "Twas you, you know it, as much as I. Besides, what use in talking? Listen to me: 'tis but six o'clock. There's money to cross the water: such as they can't follow. Yarmouth's not so far, and most night boats sail for Holland, I've heard. See you to the horses. I can be ready.'

Joseph stared at her. 'What will they say here?'

'What? Why, cannot you tell the parson we have wind of property lying in Amsterdam which we must claim or lose? Go, go; or if you are not man enough for that, lie here again tonight.' He shivered and went.

That evening after dark a boatman lumbered into an inn on Yarmouth Quay, where a man and a woman sat, with saddle-bags on the floor by them.

'Ready, are you, mistress and gentleman?' he said. 'She sails before the hour, and my other passenger he's waitin' on the quay. Be there all your baggage?' and he picked up the bags.

'Yes, we travel light,' said Joseph. 'And you have more company bound for Holland?'

'Just the one,' said the boatman, 'and he seem to travel lighter yet.'

'Do you know him?' said Madam Bowles: she laid her hand on Joseph's arm, and they both paused in the doorway.

'Why no, but for all he's hooded I'd know him again fast enough, he have such a cur'ous way of speakin', and I doubt you'll find he know you, by what he said. "Go you and fetch 'em out," he say, "and I'll wait on 'em here," he say, and sure enough he's a-comin' this way now.'

Poisoning of a husband was petty treason then, and women guilty of it were strangled at the stake and burnt. The Assize records of Norwich tell of a woman so dealt with and of her son hanged thereafter, convict on their own confession, made before the Rector of their parish, the name of which I withhold, for there is still hid treasure to be found there.

Bishop Moore's book of recipes is now in the University Library at Cambridge, marked Dd 11, 45, and on the leaf numbered 144 this is written:

An experiment most ofte proved true, to find out tresure hidden in the ground, theft, manslaughter, or anie other thynge. Go to the grave of a ded man, and three tymes call hym by his nam at the hed of the grave, and say. Thou, N., N., N., I coniure the, I require the, and I charge the, by thi Christendome that thou takest leave of the Lord Raffael and Nares and then askest leave this night to come and tell me trewlie of the tresure that lyith hid in such a place. Then take of the earth of the grave at the dead bodyes hed and knitt it in a lynnen clothe and put itt under thi right eare and sleape theruppon: and wheresoever thou lyest or slepest, that night he will come and tell thee trewlie in waking or sleping.

74

# THE MALICE OF INANIMATE OBJECTS

The Malice of Inanimate Objects is a subject upon which an old friend of mine was fond of dilating, and not without justification. In the lives of all of us, short or long, there have been days, dreadful days, on which we have had to acknowledge with gloomy resignation that our world has turned against us. I do not mean the human world of our relations and friends: to enlarge on that is the province of nearly every modern novelist. In their books it is called 'Life' and an odd enough harsh it is as they portray it. No, it is the world of things that do not speak or work or hold congresses and conferences. It includes such beings as the collar stud, the inkstand, the fire, the razor, and, as age increases, the extra step on the staircase which leads you either to expect or not to expect it. By these and such as these (for I have named but the merest fraction of them) the word is passed round, and the day of misery arranged. Is the tale still remembered of how the Cock and Hen went to pay a visit to Squire Korbes? How on the journey they met with and picked up a number of associates, encouraging each with the announcement:

To Squire Korbes we are going For a visit is owing.

Thus they secured the company of the Needle, the Egg, the Duck, the Cat, possibly—for memory is a little treacherous here—and finally the Millstone: and when it was discovered that Squire Korbes was for the moment out, they took up positions in his mansion and awaited his return. He did return, wearied no doubt by a day's work among his extensive properties. His nerves were first jarred by the raucous cry of the Cock. He threw himself into his armchair and was lacerated by the Needle. He went to the sink for a refreshing wash and was splashed all over by the Duck. Attempting to dry himself with the towel he broke the Egg upon his face.

He suffered other indignities from the Hen and her accomplices, which I cannot now recollect, and finally, maddened with pain and fear, rushed out by the back door and had his brains dashed out by the Millstone that had perched itself in the appropriate place. 'Truly,' in the concluding words of the story, 'this Squire Korbes must have been either a very wicked or a very unfortunate man.' It is the latter alternative which I incline to accept. There is nothing in the preliminaries to show that any slur rested on his name, or that his visitors had any injury to avenge. And will not this narrative serve as a striking example of that Malice of which I have taken upon me to treat? It is, I know, the fact that Squire Korbes's visitors were not all of them, strictly speaking, inanimate. But are we sure that the perpetrators of this Malice are really inanimate either? There are tales which seem to justify a doubt.

Two men of mature years were seated in a pleasant garden after breakfast. One was reading the day's paper, the other sat with folded arms, plunged in thought, and on his face were a piece of sticking plaster and lines of care. His companion lowered his paper. 'What,' said he, 'is the matter with you? The morning is bright, the birds are singing, I can hear no aeroplanes or motor bikes.'

'No,' replied Mr Burton, 'it is nice enough, I agree, but I have a

76

bad day before me. I cut myself shaving and spilt my tooth powder.'

'Ah,' said Mr Manners, 'some people have all the luck,' and with this expression of sympathy he reverted to his paper. 'Hullo,' he exclaimed, after a moment, 'here's George Wilkins dead! You won't have any more bother with him, anyhow.'

'George Wilkins?' said Mr Burton, more than a little excitedly, 'Why, I didn't even know he was ill.'

'No more he was, poor chap. Seems to have thrown up the sponge and put an end to himself. Yes,' he went on, 'it's some days back: this is the inquest. Seemed very much worried and depressed, they say. What about, I wonder?

'Could it have been that will you and he were having a row about?'

'Row?' said Mr Burton angrily, 'there was no row: he hadn't a leg to stand on: he couldn't bring a scrap of evidence. No, it may have been half-a-dozen things: but Lord! I never imagined he'd take anything so hard as that.'

'I don't know,' said Mr Manners, 'he was a man, I thought, who did take things hard: they rankled. Well, I'm sorry, though I never saw much of him. He must have gone through a lot to make him cut his throat. Not the way I should choose, by a long sight. Ugh! Lucky he hadn't a family, anyhow. Look here, what about a walk round before lunch? I've an errand in the village.'

Mr Burton assented rather heavily. He was perhaps reluctant to give the inanimate objects of the district a chance of getting at him. If so, he was right. He just escaped a nasty purl over the scraper at the top of the steps: a thorny branch swept off his hat and scratched his fingers, and as they climbed a grassy slope he fairly leapt into the air with a cry and came down flat on his face. 'What in the world?' said his friend coming up. 'A great string, of all things! What business—Oh, I see—belongs to that kite' (which lay on the grass a little farther up). 'Now if I can find out what little beast has left that kicking about, I'll let him have it—or rather I won't, for he shan't see his kite again. It's rather a good one, too.' As they approached, a puff of wind raised the kite and it seemed to sit up on its end and look at them with two large round eyes painted red, and, below them, three large printed red letters, I.C.U. Mr Manners was amused and scanned the device with care. 'Ingenious,' he said, 'it's a bit off a poster, of course: I see! Full Particulars, the word was.' Mr Burton on the other hand was not amused, but thrust his stick through the kite. Mr Manners was inclined to regret this. 'I dare say it serves him right,' he said, 'but he'd taken a lot of trouble to make it.'

'Who had?' said Mr Burton sharply. 'Oh, I see, you mean the boy.'

'Yes, to be sure, who else? But come on down now: I want to leave a message before lunch.' As they turned a corner into the main street, a rather muffled and choky voice was heard to say 'Look out! I'm coming.' They both stopped as if they had been shot.

'Who was that?' said Manners. 'Blest if I didn't think I knew'— then, with almost a yell of laughter he pointed with his stick. A cage with a grey parrot in it was hanging in an open window across the way. 'I was startled, by George: it gave you a bit of a turn, too, didn't it?' Burton was inaudible. 'Well,

I shan't be a minute: you can go and make friends with the bird.' But when he rejoined Burton, that unfortunate was not, it seemed, in trim for talking with either birds or men; he was some way ahead and going rather quickly. Manners paused for an instant at the parrot window and then hurried on laughing more than ever. 'Have a good talk with Polly?' said he, as he came up.

'No, of course not,' said Burton, testily. 'I didn't bother about the beastly thing.'

'Well, you wouldn't have got much out of her if you'd tried,' said Manners. 'I remembered after a bit; they've had her in the window for years: she's stuffed.' Burton seemed about to make a remark, but suppressed it.

Decidedly this was not Burton's day out. He choked at lunch, he broke a pipe, he tripped in the carpet, he dropped his book in the pond in the garden. Later on he had or professed to have a telephone call summoning him back to town next day and cutting short what should have been a week's visit. And so glum was he all the evening that Manners' disappointment in losing an ordinarily cheerful companion was not very sharp.

At breakfast Mr Burton said little about his night: but he did intimate that he thought of looking in on his doctor. 'My hand's so shaky,' he said, 'I really daren't shave this morning.'

'Oh, I'm sorry,' said Mr Manners, 'my man could have managed that for you: but they'll put you right in no time.'

Farewells were said. By some means and for some reason Mr Burton contrived to reserve a compartment to himself. (The train was not of the corridor type.) But these precautions avail little against the angry dead.

I will not put dots or stars, for I dislike them, but I will say that apparently someone tried to shave Mr Burton in the train, and did not succeed overly well. He was however satisfied with what he had done, if we may judge from the fact that on a once white napkin spread on Mr Burton's chest was an inscription in red letters: GEO. W. FECI.

Do not these facts—if facts they are—bear out my suggestion that there is something not inanimate behind the Malice of Inanimate Objects? Do they not further suggest that when this malice begins to show itself we should be very particular to examine and if possible rectify any obliquities in our recent conduct? And do they not, finally, almost force upon us the conclusion that, like Squire Korbes, Mr Burton must have been either a very wicked or a singularly unfortunate man?

# A VIGNETTE

You are asked to think of the spacious garden of a country
rectory, adjacent to a park of many acres, and separated
therefrom by a belt of trees of some age which we knew as the
Plantation. It is but about thirty or forty yards broad. A close
gate of split oak leads to it from the path encircling the
garden, and when you enter it from that side you put your
hand through a square hole cut in it and lift the hook to pass
along to the iron gate which admits to the park from the
Plantation. It has further to be added that from some
windows of the rectory, which stands on a somewhat lower
level than the Plantation, parts of the path leading thereto,
and the oak gate itself can be seen. Some of the trees, Scotch
firs and others, which form a backing and a surrounding, are
of considerable size, but there is nothing that diffuses a
mysterious gloom or imparts a sinister flavour—nothing of
melancholy or funereal associations. The place is well clad,
and there are secret nooks and retreats among the bushes, but
there is neither offensive bleakness nor oppressive darkness.
It is, indeed, a matter for some surprise when one thinks it
over, that any cause for misgivings of a nervous sort have
attached itself to so normal and cheerful a spot, the more so,
since neither our childish mind when we lived there nor the
more inquisitive years that came later ever nosed out any
legend or reminiscence of old or recent unhappy things.
Yet to me they came, even to me, leading an exceptionally
happy wholesome existence, and guarded—not strictly but as

carefully as was any way necessary—from uncanny fancies and fear. Not that such guarding avails to close up all gates. I should be puzzled to fix the date at which any sort of misgiving about the Plantation gate first visited me. Possibly it was in the years just before I went to school, possibly on one later summer afternoon of which I have a faint memory, when I was coming back after solitary roaming in the park, or, as I bethink me, from tea at the Hall: anyhow, alone, and fell in with one of the villagers also homeward bound just as I was about to turn off the road on to the track leading to the Plantation. We broke off our talk with 'good nights', and when I looked back at him after a minute or so I was just a little surprised to see him standing still and looking after me. But no remark passed, and on I went. By the time I was within the iron gate and outside the park, dusk had undoubtedly come on; but there was no lack yet of light, and I could not account to myself for the questionings which certainly did rise as to the presence of anyone else among the trees, questionings to which I could not very certainly say 'No', nor, I was glad to feel, 'Yes', because if there were anyone they could not well have any business there. To be sure, it is difficult, in anything like a grove, to be quite certain that nobody is making a screen out of a tree trunk and keeping it between you and him as he moves round it and you walk on. All I can say is that if such an one was there he was no neighbour or acquaintance of mine, and there was some indication about him of being cloaked or hooded. But I think I may have moved at a rather quicker pace than before, and have been particular about shutting the gate. I think, too, that after that evening something of what Hamlet calls a 'gain-giving' may have been present in my mind when I thought of the Plantation, I do seem to remember looking out of a window which gave in that direction, and questioning whether there was or was not any appearance of a moving form among the trees. If I did, and perhaps I did, hint a suspicion to the nurse the only answer to it will have been 'the hidea of such a thing!' and an injunction to make haste and get into my bed.

Whether it was on that night or a later one that I seem to see myself again in the small hours gazing out of the window across moonlit grass and hoping I was mistaken in fancying any movement in that half-hidden corner of the garden, I cannot now be sure. But it was certainly within a short while that I began to be visited by dreams which I would much rather not have had—which, in fact, I came to dread acutely; and the point round which they centred was the Plantation gate.

As years go on it but seldom happens that a dream is disturbing. Awkward it may be, as when, while I am drying myself after a bath, I open the bedroom door and step out on to a populous railway platform and have to invent rapid and flimsy excuses for the deplorable deshabille. But such a vision is not alarming, though it may make one despair of ever holding up one's head again. But in the times of which I am thinking, it did happen, not often, but oftener than I liked, that the moment a dream set in I knew that it was going to turn out ill, and that there was nothing I could do to keep it on cheerful lines.

Ellis the gardener might be wholesomely employed with rake and spade as I watched at the window; other familiar figures might pass and repass on harmless errands; but I was not deceived. I could see that the time was coming when the gardener and the rest would be gathering up their properties and setting off on paths that led homeward or into some safe outer world, and the garden would be left—to itself, shall we say, or to denizens who did not desire quite ordinary company and were only waiting for the word 'all clear' to slip into their posts of vantage.

Now, too, was the moment near when the surroundings began to take on a threatening look; that the sunlight lost power and a quality of light replaced it which, though I did not know it at the time my memory years after told me was the lifeless pallor of an eclipse. The effect of all this was to intensify the foreboding that had begun to possess me, and to make me look anxiously about, dreading that in some quarter my fear would take a visible shape. I had not much doubt which way to look. Surely behind those bushes, among those trees, there was motion, yes, and surely—and more quickly than seemed possible—there was motion, not now among the trees, but on the very path towards the house. I was still at the window, and before I could adjust myself to the new fear there came the impression of a tread on the stairs and a hand on the door. That was as far as the dream got, at first; and for me it was far enough. I had no notion what would have been the next development, more than that it was bound to be horrifying.

That is enough in all conscience about the beginning of my dreams. A beginning it was only, for something like it came again and again; how often I can't tell, but often enough to give me an acute distaste for being left alone in that region of the garden. I came to fancy that I could see in the behaviour of the village people whose work took them that way an anxiety to be past a certain point, and moreover a welcoming of company as they approached that corner of the park. But on this it will not do to lay overmuch stress, for, as I have said, I could never glean any kind of story bound up with the place.

84

However, the strong probability that there had been one once I cannot deny.

I must not by the way give the impression that the whole of the Plantation was haunted ground. There were trees there most admirably devised for climbing and reading in; there was a wall, along the top of which you could walk for many hundred yards and reach a frequented road, passing farmyard and familiar houses; and once in the park, which had its own delights of wood and water, you were well out of range of anything suspicious—or, if that is too much to say, of anything that suggested the Plantation gate.

But I am reminded, as I look on these pages, that so far we have had only preamble, and that there is very little in the way of actual incident to come, and that the criticism attributed to the devil when he sheared the sow is like to be justified. What, after all, was the outcome of the dreams to which without saying a word about them I was liable during a good space of time? Well, it presents itself to me thus. One afternoon—the day being neither overcast nor threatening—I was at my window in the upper floor of the house. All the family were out. From some obscure shelf in a disused room I had worried out a book, not very recondite: it was, in fact, a bound volume of a magazine in which were contained parts of a novel. I know now what novel it was, but I did not then, and a sentence struck and arrested me. Someone was walking at dusk up a solitary lane by an old mansion in Ireland, and being a man of imagination he was suddenly forcibly impressed by what he calls 'the aerial image of the old house, with its peculiar malign, scared, and skulking aspect' peering out of the shade of its neglected old trees. The words were quite enough to set my own fancy on a bleak track. Inevitably I looked and looked with apprehension, to the Plantation gate. As was but right it was shut, and nobody was upon the path that led to it or from it. But as I said a while ago, there was in it a square hole giving access to the fastening; and through that hole, I could see—and it struck like a blow on the diaphragm—something white or partly white. Now this I could not bear, and with an access of something like courage—only it was more like desperation, like determining that I must know the worst—I did steal down and, quite uselessly, of course, taking cover behind bushes as I went, I made progress until I was within range of the gate and the hole. Things were, alas! worse than I had feared; through that hole a face was looking my way. It was not monstrous, not pale, fleshless, spectral. Malevolent I thought and think it was; at any rate the eyes were large and open and fixed. It was pink and, I thought, hot, and just above the eyes the border of a white linen drapery hung down from the brows.

There is something horrifying in the sight of a face looking at one out of a frame as this did; more particularly if its gaze is unmistakably fixed upon you. Nor does it make the matter any better if the expression gives no clue to what is to come next. I said just now that I took this face to be malevolent, and so I did, but not in regard of any positive dislike or fierceness which it expressed. It was, indeed, quite without emotion: I was only conscious that I could see the whites of the eyes all round the pupil, and that, we know, has a glamour of madness about it. The immovable face was enough for me. I fled, but at what I thought must be a safe distance inside my own precincts I could not but halt and look back. There was no white thing framed in the hole of the gate, but there was a draped form shambling away among the trees.

Do not press me with questions as to how I bore myself when it became necessary to face my family again. That I was upset by something I had seen must have been pretty clear, but I am very sure that I fought off all attempts to describe it. Why I make a lame effort to do it now I cannot very well explain: it undoubtedly has had some formidable power of clinging through many years to my imagination. I feel that even now I should be circumspect in passing that Plantation gate; and every now and again the query haunts me: Are there here and there sequestered places which some curious creatures still frequent, whom once on a time anybody could see and speak to as they went about on their daily occasions, whereas now only at rare intervals in a series of years does one cross their paths and become aware of them; and perhaps that is just as well for the peace of mind of simple people.

www.ingramcontent.com/pod-product-compliance
Lightning Source LLC
Chambersburg PA
CBHW011441170626
46807CB00008B/3257